My Husband's Adventures

My Husband's Adventures

Confessions from the Wife of a Cuckold Bull

ALEX HATHAWAY

Seattle, WA

fannypress

Fanny Press
PO Box 70515
Seattle, WA 98127

For more information go to: www.fannypress.com

This is a work of fiction. Names, characters, places, brands, media, and incidents are either the product of the author's imagination or are used fictitiously.

Cover design by Sabrina Sun

My Husband's Adventures
Copyright © 2016 by Alex Hathaway

ISBN: 978-1-60381-601-4 (Trade Paper)
ISBN: 978-1-60381-602-1 (eBook)

Printed in the United States of America

Also by the author

From Housewife to Cuckoldress

Education of a Cuckold

Chapter 1

———

As girls turn into teens, we fantasize about gallant husbands who make us weak in their arms. Somewhere along the way, we think about children. We wonder if the same men who sweep us off our feet can be the ones to calm the baby at 4 a.m. and have the sack lunches ready. Doubt creeps in as we start dating. Eventually, it dawns on us: it's hard enough to find a great lover, much less a lifetime companion.

Well, I found a husband. And he fit the bill on almost every count. But it wasn't enough. We lost our way, and almost lost our marriage. Then we found our way back again—I think. As for how we did it … well, I can't think of a single therapist who would support it.

I don't have anyone I can tell the whole story to, so I thought I'd write it down here. If you're reading this, I took it further than I ever expected.

I met my future husband when I was twenty-three. I was in love with another man at the time—or so I thought. The other man, Daniel, even bought me a ring, though he hadn't proposed. I found the ring in his sock drawer.

I'm reluctant to tell you much about myself physically; I'm not sure it really matters. I'm pretty tall, about five feet nine. White, though my skin browns reliably in the summer. You can put your pornographic fantasies away, because I don't have huge tits or anything like that. I've always worn a B cup and wished my breasts were bigger. I envy women who have breasts that dangle confidently in front of them, even if time can be cruel to the danglier ones.

When I was thirteen, I thought I was going to have huge breasts—much to my mother's consternation. She even took me to a doctor to talk about how I might cope, socially and medically, if my breasts got bigger. She had constant back problems by the age of forty due to the size of her bosom. But after I reached the age of fifteen, my breasts did not get any bigger. That was me, fully grown.

Even though I topped out early, having large breasts for my age educated me into the ways of men early. I got used to swatting men like flies. I soon learned that the more ruthless and dismissive I could be, the better off I was. Guys had a tendency to read "yes" into every smile I gave them.

I recently found a picture of myself in a bikini at age sixteen. I remember how awkward I felt in that bikini, with its itchy red fabric, nothing like the sex symbol men seemed to think I was at the time; I was uncomfortable in my bones. What stands out for me in that picture is how wide my hips were—nothing like a little girl's hips. A few years later, my first serious boyfriend would refer to "your impossible curves." It made me red in the face.

How I looked then or now shouldn't matter, but there *is* something you should know. I've always been aware of a certain power I had over men—most men, anyway. I've always despised the girls who used that power to their advantage. So I tried not to … most of the time.

At age sixteen, I didn't really dress in the shorter skirts or tight jeans of my friends. My pants were mostly baggy. I thought that if I went for a tight fit, my wide hips would make me look fat.

I was always damn good at math. I soaked up every math class I could, even taking geometry and algebra in the same year as a sophomore. It was the only way I would get all the way to calculus before graduating. I was the only girl in my class to complete our math curriculum with straight As.

Taking those classes put me in contact with some freaks and geeks; I felt right at home. Eventually they got used to me. Most of my best friends, male and female, came from that geekier crowd. Already outcasts, they weren't afraid to be seen as smart. They were happy skipping a kegger to go to an all-night diner and talk about *Doctor Who* versus *Star Trek*, or even serious shit like pill-popping dads or alcoholic moms.

If I'm giving you the impression I was a bookworm, that's not right either. I dated a lot of guys, but I went about it quietly. I learned a sneaky trick from older girls in my town: be friends with guys from your school, but date guys from other schools. This strategy protected you from the worst of the rumor mill. It worked especially well for girls like me who didn't just want to kiss guys, but wanted to *fuck*.

I was considered a conservative girl around my school, which helped me get away with whatever I wanted outside of it. Even in college, I played it that way. There were two colleges nearby in Vermont where I went to school, so I would date off campus and keep that part of my life more private.

By college, I wasn't as awkward. I had figured out how to get my sexual needs met. But I had already decided one thing about a career: I didn't want to use my slinky charm to take me further professionally. And no, I didn't sleep with any professors.

I wanted to earn my stripes. After graduating, I refused a job my roommate got me through her parents. I moved to San Francisco instead and found my own way. I got hired as an Accenture consultant-in-training and began a successful career in predictive analytics, which is all the rage in business circles these days. Companies don't just want to know they have a leak; they want to know why. They want to know how they can predict what their customers will want to buy next—and I can help them. My ability to wear a power suit and work a room filled with stiffs comes in handy too. Eventually, I turned those skills into a sales role—technically, it's called pre-sales. I bring the meat *and* the charm.

There is one really big change about me professionally, though. These days, I am totally confident in my brain power as the source of my achievement. As a result, I am not afraid to assert myself sexually.

I don't dress provocatively, but I do wear power suits that are custom fitted—usually with skirts that accentuate my hips down into my legs, which stay muscular enough thanks to my gym rat tendencies. Wow, I sound like a superficial brat right now, sorry.

I still have some insecurities about my body; I *do* miss the competitive swimmer muscle tone I had when I was eighteen. But all powered up in my work suits, I know my hips/ass/legs are still imposing to men. I like seeing them stutter and avoid eye contact when I am speaking or presenting. I can tell they are wondering if they could ever please a woman like me. When I see that "she's out of my league" doubt on their faces, I give them a stern look over my wire-framed glasses, as if to say, "Yeah, you don't have a shot. And don't bother trying."

I was a bit of a slut in college, of the unashamed variety. But after college, I had an emotional relapse. By that I mean, I started to crave a deeper connection to the men in my life. I wanted to feel close; I wanted to feel taken care of. I'm not sure what caused that. Maybe it was the uncertainty of my post-college existence and being far away from my best girlfriends. Maybe it was because my father died when I was twenty-one, leaving me disoriented.

I reverted into a snuggle bunny. I dated geeky guys who

weren't afraid to just be with me, whether we had sex or not. I liked guys who would listen, who would write me poetry or dedicate songs to me at open mics. I liked guys who could cook a great omelet and who were secure enough to be completely happy eating pussy all night long, not fucking at all if I didn't feel like it.

Then, at twenty-three years old, I met my future husband, and that was the end of all that.

Chapter 2

WHEN I MET MY future husband, Jackson, I was already engaged to a lovely young man—the aforementioned Daniel. Daniel was a PhD film student who taught me about the history of cinema. Not to mention gave me some of the best fingering I ever had. The cliché is that girls love oral sex, but let me tell you, a guy who can work his fingers is heaven. Daniel definitely had magic fingers.

We were very much in love … or so I told myself. Daniel told me all his secrets; he cried in my arms over the loss of his kid brother. For me, it was my father, and my struggle to move on from a man who was no longer alive but whose stern looks and impossibly high standards still weighed heavily.

Daniel was a beautiful person inside and out; I could imagine spending the rest of my life with him. He carried my secrets so well—most of them anyway. But there was one secret he didn't know. Poor Daniel. Jackson knew that secret the moment he first saw me.

Daniel was a skinny dude with bushy red hair. His indifference to his appearance was part of his charm. I was hardly the only girl who found his modern-geek-meets-throwback-gentleman mix catchy. But I wasn't concerned about the other girls. I had blown Daniel's mind enough times in the sack to have him right where I wanted him.

In the summer of 2001, Daniel got a teaching job in Toronto. For PhD candidates, those early teaching gigs are crucial. You don't bicker about location—you go where the work is. Daniel was ecstatic. Teaching film to high school students would be a blast; he planned to sneak in three weeks on horror and three weeks on science fiction appreciation. More importantly, those who taught at this program often found their way into big-time teaching positions down the road. You could make great contacts there.

As a traveling consultant working part-time out of Boston and the rest on the road, I figured I could visit Daniel often. It wasn't hard to fly in and out. So Daniel left town and left me to my own devices, which I thought would mostly be working, traveling, and eating solitary frozen dinners.

Then, at a ridiculous party, everything changed.

I WAS ONLY THERE to pick up my friend Montana. It was some kind of birthday party for who the hell knows. Montana was not around when I knocked. A hippie-looking girl blowing on a kazoo welcomed me in.

I wandered down a hallway, Jay-Z pounding through distorted speakers. In the kitchen, I saw Jackson. I'm not sure I can describe this without making you laugh, but even at first glance, I was overpowered by the force of his masculinity. Jackson was a strong-looking, squared-jawed son of a bitch with light-brown skin and a twinkle in his eye. I can't even tell you why he had this power, because he didn't say much of anything to me.

I looked Jackson in the eye, and he stared me down without the slightest hint of intimidation. I knew instantly I would be spreading my legs for him. The shocks in between my thighs could have powered a shopping mall Christmas tree. Five minutes later, when Jackson matter-of-factly asked me for my phone number in front of about ten people, I scribbled it down with a urgency that must have looked incredibly slutty. For the first time in my life, I actually felt my pussy leak from being hit on.

I handed him my number in front of all those people and blushed like crazy, but it was done. Two nights later, Jackson was giving me the best orgasms of my life. I surrendered my pussy to him with complete abandon—a far cry from the painfully slow courtship I put Daniel through.

Two hours into our first time together, I was lying next to Jackson, dripping in sweat. I was still coming down from wailing orgasms that must have been a real treat for my condo neighbors. I suddenly had this horrible (and horribly true) thought:

You and Daniel have made love many times, but you have never really fucked—not like THIS.

Ugh. Jackson and I fucked every night I was in town for the next month. I even called in sick three days in a row, something I never do. Also: I figured out excuses not to visit Daniel.

A month into Jackson, I was washing dishes, savoring that well-fucked feeling throughout my entire body, loosey-goosey and happy as all get out. Then I had a moment. Daniel was due to call that night.

Sadness flooded me. What would I say? I had never talked to Jackson about whether we were even dating. As far as he knew, we were sport fucking. We'd been out of the house together only once—I didn't want to waste his magnificent body on dinner conversation. Daniel, though … I was still engaged to Daniel. Or about to be. He owned my heart.

Then I had another one of those terrible, dirty thoughts:

But how can Daniel own your heart if Jackson owns your pussy?

Jackson *did* own my pussy. I could always hold my own with

Daniel in bed. But Jackson could simply reach in and scoop my orgasms out, leaving me quivering in his wake.

Like most girls in my situation, I assumed Jackson was a slutty phase I would soon grow out of, like that decadent banana split you gorge on until you are repulsed.

So I did what any sensible career woman would do: I told Jackson I was about to be engaged, kicked him out of my life with a big, regretful kiss, and tried to put that episode behind me.

A third of the way through the summer, Daniel managed to get a long weekend off from his summer course. Maybe he was nervous. Maybe he sensed something. He found his way home.

The weird thing was, after all the great lovemaking we had done, we both tried to *fuck* that night. Daniel literally ripped my clothes off, even tearing my good work blouse. Instead of his usual expert foreplay, within a couple of minutes he was pushing his dick inside me.

The fuck didn't go that well. Daniel had a difficult time staying hard. Without the foreplay, my pussy was dry. He had trouble getting inside me. With Jackson, I had been so wet the first time we fucked that my panties were soaked before they came off.

Prior to that bad sex with Daniel, I had never thought much about penis size. Sure, I had a few female friends who were crazy about big dicks. And sometimes I joined in the laughing stories of the little-dicked guys we had the misfortune of sharing beds with.

But I always had a soft spot for the little guys. Many were really sweet, and there were plenty of things to enjoy besides fucking … take Daniel and his magic fingers. Nor did the size issue really bother me. It was just something to joke about with my girlfriends, or a way to make fun of jerks who were likely overcompensating.

But that night, once Daniel managed to get himself erect

and we started fucking, I couldn't really feel him. I flashed to Jackson's big thick penis, and how from the second he put that thick head inside me, I was intensely, blissfully aware that I was being *fucked*. God, I missed that feeling. But did I miss it enough to wreck my life?

Before Jackson, it had been a long time since I had fucked a big cock. In college, I was always experimenting with different things, even anal, and I was afraid of taking something too big in there. I prided myself on being sexually compatible with anyone I was attracted to—male or female. If two people wanted each other, you just had to be creative.

Yet looking down at Daniel pounding away without result, I found myself thinking about Jackson, wishing it was his big cock stretching me open. It occurred to me that even at this moment, another girl was likely screaming and cumming all over Jackson's big penis. I felt a flash of anger and resentment. The resulting months were chaos.

A year later, Jackson was putting a ring on my finger. A year after that, we were married. A year later, a baby girl, Chelsea, or "Chels" as we call her. Our first and so far, our only. She's eight years old now, and pure spitfire. Fortunately she is the school's problem for seven hours a day, longer when she has drum practice. Yes, she plays the drum in the marching band. It's the only band of its kind in the country that I know of, at least for kids her age.

And no, breaking things off with Daniel did not go well. Nor did he take it well. Frankly, I didn't blame him. I put him through hell; I'm sure I made him feel he wasn't worthy.

I still have his ring. With bitter tears, he made me take it. I wanted him to keep it for another woman, but he insisted that the "ring go down with the ship." Last time I checked, it was still in my sock drawer, an homage that underneath his anger, I think Daniel would appreciate.

You may wonder why I left the love of my live for my sexual crush. You're not the only one. Most of my girlfriends thought

I was nuts. But it wasn't that simple. After three months of seeing Jackson as much as possible, I told him I loved him. Well, actually, I told him I loved him about three weeks into our relationship, but that was when his cock was making my pussy scream with happiness. I made a point of taking those words back immediately, after all that cumming was over, letting him know I spoke out of sexual joy and not from the heart. I was still trying to save that part of my body for Daniel.

Jackson laughed when I told him that. Noting how my arms leaned submissively on his barrel chest, he probably didn't worry too much about my devotion. The amused look on his face pretty much said, "I'll get you in time." Three months later, he did. By then, Daniel and I were in hot water anyhow; angry long-distance phone conversations had become the norm. He knew something was amiss.

Chapter 3

HERE'S HOW I FELL completely in love with Jackson. About three months after we first had sex, I heard an unexpected knock at my door. I thought maybe it was Daniel, back in town to find out what the fuck was going on and stare me down.

But it was actually Jackson, showing up at my house to take me to a party for the first time as his guest (we still hadn't gone out on the town much). It was a 1920s party, and he was dressed to the nines, with blinking red suspenders. I'm not even sure they wore suspenders in the '20s, but he looked awesome.

Jackson waited in the living room while I rustled through closets for an outfit. I managed to rustle up an old school Tango-style dance outfit. That probably wasn't the twenties either, but it had a classic look. When I came downstairs, Jackson produced some rose petals and gently tacked them to my blouse. And with that gesture, he flipped the switch.

It wasn't just that he thought to bring flowers. It was the way he gently put them on, with that sweet look on his face that betrayed his respect. He was my lover, and he was my protector. He had me. Jackson grabbed my hand and led me to his car.

"Wait!"

I pulled him to me, kissing him as hard as I've ever kissed anyone. It was less romantic than possessive. I knew right then, pulling him to me in my front yard, that he was my future husband. Daniel and I were done. I called him and broke up the very next day.

I had girlfriends who looked down upon sexual fulfillment as the basis of my marriage, but I could see their jealousy also. I could see their faces flush when I got off Jackson's lap in a crowded bar, his trousers unable to conceal his big swollen penis.

All I know is that when things aren't going well with your spouse, having someone who can fuck you into another universe isn't a bad thing. In Jackson's case, he's also a really good guy. No, I don't love him quite the way I loved Daniel, but replacing that tenderness is an animal fascination that never fully resolves itself. And raising a child with Jackson, we are bound together.

If my pairing with Daniel was more enlightened, my marriage with Jackson goes back to a time when men were men and women were women, but with some important distinctions. Such as: he has never laid a hand on me in anger.

It took me seven more years of marriage to realize just how good I have it. Finding a husband who is as powerful a lover as he is a wonderful father and provider … that's damn near impossible. I know that because of all the girlfriends who have sobbed into cheap daiquiris and spilled the stories of their marriages to me.

But as good as I have it, and as good as I still get it, Jackson and I have our share of problems. Serious problems. Sexy problems, but problems that can wreck a marriage nonetheless. And may yet wreck mine. But that's what I have to confess to you.

In truth, I could see the seeds of those problems from the beginning. Jackson, well, he was a little too perfect, I guess you could say.

Chapter 4

IT ALL STARTED DURING that first summer, when I was still spending so much time horizontally with Jackson, trying to keep my emotional thread with Daniel in Toronto after our weekend of bad sex. It was one of those miraculous days in bed with Jackson. I woke up flat on my back, in a sexual nether zone between asleep and awake.

Jackson had fucked me out of my mind; my legs were jelly. I hit the snooze alarm to postpone my white collar reckoning, but I didn't think I could get up anyway. Cashing in a sick day was a distinct possibility. I always enjoy the quiet times after Jackson leaves for work. He runs a landscaping franchise and always has his guys up early, terrorizing neighborhoods with 7 a.m. weed-whackers.

"Just don't take a job on my street," I jokingly warn him. If there's one thing I'm *not*, it's not a morning person. Espresso is not a luxury in my household.

Anyhow, I was lying in bed, daydreaming about anything to block out the chaotic project I had to corral in a couple of hours. I could feel the post-orgasmic relaxation deep in my body, as if I'd been given a full body massage from the inside out.

My god, he's a good lay, I thought as I spread a bit wider under the covers. *And he's all mine*, was my next thought. But then I caught myself:

He's not yours. You've told him you're engaged. Whatever he does on his own time is ... his business.

That thought displeased me greatly.

He's not all yours.

Suddenly, that seemed like a very dark possibility. But the more I thought about it, the more I realized the truth of it. *He's not all yours, no—and it gets worse:*

Other women are as wet for him as you are; those sluts must be constantly plotting to get him between their legs.

I started touching myself compulsively, thinking about Jackson landscaping his way through the day.

He tried to conceal his bulge with baggy pants, but it was often a losing battle. I could just imagine horny housewives stealing glances at him doing manly things in their backyards, his big soft penis pushing arrogantly down his pant leg. Ironically, given his landscaping trade, Jackson was a "shower," not a grower. Perhaps that was good for business, but it made me crazy.

The contrast between the stale sex weekend with Daniel and Jackson's electric performances made me rethink my college days. I worked my fingers teasingly into my pussy as I thought back to a dude named Linwood.

Linwood was the last guy I'd dated who was as sexually talented as Jackson—or at least in the same universe of stud. Linwood had to fight women off continuously; I was starting to fear the same was true of Jackson. Linwood—and yes, his nickname was "The Wood"—was a guitarist who knew how to play a woman as well as he could his guitar.

My friends and I were having a lot of sex in college, but not necessarily a lot of good sex. Linwood changed all that. He was that rare guy where the reality exceeded the fantasy. You'd see him on stage in some cramped college bar, jammed up front to get a glimpse of whatever was packing in his thrift shop plaid, and you'd think, "*He must be too stoned to really deliver the goods.*" But he was not. Linwood could grind, and word got around. I thought that was hilarious at the time. But as I got more emotionally attached, "hilarious" was not the word that came to mind.

Linwood and I dated for a few months. I wasn't serious about him, but his inability to stay faithful did eventually get under my skin. Linwood did his best, but he could only fight them off for so long. Linwood was charming and sheepish when caught in a lie, shrugging his shoulders as if to say, *It's not my fault I was gifted with an exceptionally nice penis, a long tongue, and silky hips.*

I didn't appreciate his flings, but on some level that's all he and I were having: one big fling. So despite the occasional indignation, I put up with Linwood's infidelities, until the day I came home from a failed midterm and found him nailing my roommate to her mattress. My roommate was ultra-competitive with me, and that was a line I wasn't willing to cross—or have crossed. I gave Linwood the boot.

My roommate at the time—I guess we all have a roommate named Jessica at some point in college—was apologetic.

"He's just so much ... *better* than my boyfriend," she admitted. Jessica's boyfriend was an uptight pre-law guy, a classic case of fast-forwarding into adulthood and missing out on the wild years he could have had. Things were tense between Jessica and me for a while, but she had that Southern drawl and honest regret. We eventually mended fences and we're in touch to this day.

After a few years of mediocre sexual encounters post-college, my feelings of betrayal toward Linwood started to fade in favor of an appreciation of the deep pleasure he had given my body. He was the first man who could take me to levels of physical ecstasy beyond what I could achieve with my own fingers. I suppose I resented him for that; it gnawed at my notion of female independence.

So I WAS LYING in bed contemplating the dilemma of Linwood, and now, Jackson. As I casually rubbed myself, and soon much less casually, I started thinking about those women—no, those *fucking sluts*—who must be homing in on Jackson. We had not been out in public much, so for now, these rampant thoughts were more in the realm of foreboding/red hot fantasies.

Jackson's not the most handsome guy, but he's big and strong and wonderfully indifferent. He doesn't speak often, but his silence gives him a charisma of its own. He sucks the air from a room. Unlike most guys, Jackson has that quiet swagger that says, "I can get sex whenever I want." That natural sexual authority is so uncommon in a man. When you run into it, your pussy does some crazy things.

After the breakup with Daniel, Jackson and I went out in public much more often. My worst fears were confirmed. Women came on to him a lot, regardless of how closely I stood watch. And many seemed to have a history. Jackson's phone became a fascination for me. I would make him hand it over constantly. Some of the texts I found were shocking. I had no idea girls could act this way.

Here are just a few of the text messages that popped up on Jackson's phone that fall, all from different women:

Bring that big dick over here NOWWWWW!!!! Oh—Kelly says hi. Hee hee.

I hate you! You ruined my pussy. Can you ruin me again? He is gone till Monday.

And, the kicker:

I have three hours till the babysitter has to leave. Please, I need to feel you inside me.

From September to December alone, I made Jackson flush hand-scrawled numbers of five women down the toilet. I made him save the numbers in his wallet until I flushed them down, so there would be no secrets between us.

Unlike most promiscuous (heterosexual) men, it was all about repeat customers with Jackson. It never failed. I'd leave him alone at a bar while talking with some friends. I'd cast a glance to check on him and he'd be oozing confidence, like a cobra relaxing in the sun. The women would glom onto him like honeybees. *Ugh!*

Yes, on some level it turned me on to know I had what they wanted. As Courtney Love once sang, "I want to be the girl with the most cake." But I can't emphasize enough what a trust issue this was between us.

About nine months into the monogamous phase of our relationship, the issue faded. Surprising even myself, I found I was less interested in what Jackson was texting. Not that I wasn't possessive—I was the one to press him on our engagement. When he'd get back from a day of landscaping, I'd joke, "Where's my ring?" As if he'd had time to go ring shopping with his overalls on.

One day, he did show up with a ring, and yeah, in his overalls without a shirt. Before Jackson proposed, we had a surprising conversation. He told me that while he loved me as much as he'd ever loved anyone, he'd always had trouble staying faithful.

The conversation bothered me. It resembled the typical male bullshit you can see on Jerry Springer Monday through Friday: he couldn't always resist the advances, and in his past relationships, his girlfriends didn't understand his needs. They didn't get that his feelings for them were unwavering, even when he crossed a sexual line with someone else. Jackson told me he would try, but he couldn't make any promises.

He wasn't putting that ring on my finger until I was okay with that. The way he said it was so firm, so decisive. It really shocked me that he could put it out there with so much indifference. As if he could accept me walking out on him over this. For a day, I was really pissed. And he didn't get any sex from me for a weekend, either.

But somehow, the storm passed. I would have dumped any other guy over that. But with Jackson, I really don't know. Maybe I was too in love to care. Maybe I thought I could change him, or that if I took care of his needs well enough, he wouldn't stray. I just knew I wasn't giving him up. And Jackson … he was one patient son of a bitch, as if he knew he would eventually wear me down. God, that made me crazy!

Chapter 5

O VER THE NEXT FEW months, things got even better between us and the problem faded. I had no doubt he was monogamous during that time. I told myself, "If you give him the best sex in the world, he'll never cheat." But the change ran deeper.

Jackson continued to prove himself again and again. A guys' night out was just that. If I called him and insisted he come home, he did. And not smelling of some skank either (if you haven't figured it out yet, I don't really believe in calling girls sluts and skanks. I just can't help myself when they are after my Jackson). He never seemed irritated by my controlling binges.

Jackson did it: he smoothed my rough edges. So I told him to put a ring on my finger. And he did, muddy knees on the kitchen floor, looking like a Chippendales reject. And it worked. It worked for a long time. We raised a little girl together, and for a couple of those years, he was the primary caregiver. He'd earned it.

During Chelsea's first two years, we got out of the house so infrequently, I actually came to enjoy it when other girls gave Jackson a bit of flirty attention. It spiced things up a tad during a time when we really needed it. But in the end, something always nagged at me. I couldn't put it into words. It wasn't a lack of trust. I was missing something fundamental.

There was a clue I was missing that would come back to haunt me.

The trust issue came back a bit at age thirty-one—eight years in. That was Chelsea in third grade, and us with more time on our hands. At first we took full advantage, with morning sex we never used to have time for, but arguments came more often as well.

Jackson was expanding his landscaping business into a new town. That meant less time near his home and more in the field. His commute to the new town near Burlington had more traffic and required a longer drive; I saw him less. I suppose my own work had something to do with it. I was stuck on a tough project. Maybe it was my over-active imagination, but it did seem like Jackson would call me a bit more often with a last minute delay at work or a change of plans.

The little things added up. For the first time, our sex life wasn't as good. We even saw a therapist. I'm not convinced he helped us that much, but it did force us to talk. The therapist (a man) seemed to have a small crush on Jackson, which added a comic element to the whole ordeal.

A year later, things were pretty much back on track. It didn't hurt that I was back in the gym. I had sprained my knee the previous year playing softball, of all things, and had packed on some pounds. When the weight came off and my muscle tone improved, so did my confidence. My controlling boss had temporarily given up on trying to force a role I didn't want on me, and who knows, maybe six weeks of marriage-counseling helped too.

This was part of our cycle. I'd get used to Jackson but then I would see him as new again, as the force of nature he was. Or he would melt me with a kind or casually amazing gesture, such as suggesting an unofficial "take your daughter to work" day or letting her drive the tractor as she squealed with glee.

I suppose that's why I never saw it coming. I guess I will always be mad that I missed some hints—especially since Jackson pretty much warned me from day one, as humiliating as that is to admit.

An odd coincidence brought everything to a head. I was working from home that week, in between gigs, only dropping by the office when I had to. I had a friend, Alicia, who I used to know well. She'd been on my mind. Jackson had even done some landscaping for her a year ago. Alicia was a blonde bombshell disguised as a suburban housewife, but she was rigorously faithful to her husband. It was a marriage I did not understand. Alicia was not broke; her family had sold an organic juice business to Whole Foods.

Her husband Brad reminded me a lot of Daniel. Devoted, for sure, but well, I just never picked up on any chemistry between Alicia and Brad. Lots of affection, but not many sparks.

I eventually wound up as a bridesmaid at her wedding. Sometime after that, we had a minor falling out over something too ridiculous to 'fess up to now.

Anyhow, I had been contemplating making peace with Alicia. Enough time had passed. I had been thinking about her ever since Jackson got a landscaping gig on her property. I'm not sure if Alicia was trying to make amends with me by hiring Jackson, but it got me reconsidering our stupid girl-feud.

I'll never know why I was compelled to do this, but one day, after cashing in a sick day so I could take Chelsea to an eye appointment, I made up a lunch for Jackson and his crew. For the first time in my history as a housewife, I decided to surprise my husband with a hot meal.

Pulling into the driveway, I saw Jackson's truck. No sign of him or his crew. I peeked around the ivy-lined fence. Nothing out back, either. But the glass patio door was open. Suspicious, I invited myself in. Two melting drinks on the tea table, iced teas barely touched.

And then I heard it. It sounded like a woman in distress. Banging sounds, yells. Heart pounding, I thought about calling 911. But where the fuck was Jackson? Cellphone in hand, finger on the emergency button, I moved quickly down the hallway toward the noise.

As I headed for the ruckus, I realized those noises sounded a lot more ecstatic than distressed. Still, I told myself, Alicia might be in trouble; I needed to see what I needed to see. One more corner on padded carpet, and I peeked around the bedroom door, which was wide open.

The scene was everything I'd never wanted to see. Alicia was bouncing up and down on Jackson, riding him in a frenzy. It was only later I would look back on this scene as sexy, her blonde hair caked in sweat, gripping the headboard so hard that it slammed against the wall.

Alicia spotted me in the bedroom mirror and her eyes popped, but that bitch didn't even have the courtesy to stop fucking. She was too far gone; nothing was going to stop her from riding it out. Jackson, who has a GPS-like sense of where I am in the world, whipped his head around. His eyes were sorrowful and conflicted, but he didn't try to stop Alicia; she was doing most of the fucking anyhow. I guess Jackson figured the damage was done. Alicia might as well cum for thirty more seconds.

I was so shocked by this absurdity that it took me a while to notice the most shocking thing. In the farthest corner of the room, in the shade of the curtains, Alicia's husband Brad was sitting in a folding chair, and while he was basically fully clothed, he was frantically jerking himself off. I was overwhelmed and a bit repulsed.

"Corrie!" I heard Jackson call out. But I was already out the back and gone, revving up my car. I wiped the sting from my eyes to see a blurry Jackson in my field of view, waving me down while clutching a towel. It was probably comical in a reality show kind of way, but it wasn't funny at the time.

Chapter 6

THESE DAYS, I THINK back to that incident with curiosity. No, it didn't turn me on at all. And yeah, I was frothing mad. I wanted nothing to do with Jackson sexually. And yet … I didn't kick him out of the house. I *did* ask him to sleep in the garage; he didn't even qualify for the couch.

Our daughter was confused by my actions, but she was old enough to grasp that sometimes women get really ticked off at men. Perhaps Chelsea was relieved—maybe she sensed I wasn't going to kick Jackson out, or go to a further extreme. I could see her sneaking things to Jackson—a Yoplait here, a T-shirt there. I didn't stop her.

During this pissed-off phase, Jackson seemed to know exactly how to handle me. He steered clear, getting Chelsea to fetch things from the house. He knew I was too sweet on her to stop her from running his little missions. He didn't try to make conversation, but left me the usual notes on the fridge— "I'll pick up Chelsea after band," etc. He frequently took the shopping list from our fridge clipper and brought the groceries dutifully home.

About two weeks into the silent treatment phase, I snapped

at Jackson in the kitchen. "Make your own fucking iced tea!" I believe it was. But one day later, I saw him on the front steps braiding Chelsea's hair while she waited for a ride from her pal Katie. (Jackson had learned to braid hair from his sisters, and to tell the truth, he was better at it than I was). Seeing how completely Chelsea trusted him while he sat on his milk crate and got her hair just right melted a crack in my concrete heart.

But Jackson stayed in the garage, crashing on the ratty brown couch that used to be in his collegiate cave, the one piece of crud furniture I let him keep. About a week after the front yard braiding, I had a problem with the kitchen sink. Ordinarily I would have asked Jackson to fix the leak by default, but I was still on my "I don't need that motherfucker, or any man, for that matter" kick.

I required a special wrench we kept on a peg in the garage, so I figured I would barge in on Jackson. After all, he hadn't earned any privacy.

When I walked in, I gasped. Jackson was jacking off vigorously, working both hands up and down his shaft, which he had evidently greased up with Vaseline or something. His dick looked angry and shiny, tempting me, but also scolding me for neglecting it.

I had forgotten just how big his penis looked when it was fully hard, and how embarrassingly powerless I felt around it. Before I even realized what I was doing, I hiked up my skirt and pushed Jackson back on the couch. I hated the smug look on his face—that *I knew you'd be back for this big dick* look—but there was nothing I could do about that now. I needed to cum all over him. No foreplay, and rougher than usual. I wasn't as sloppy wet as I usually am when he enters me.

As I settled down on his cock, I really struggled. Not being wet, I could feel the burn as he pushed his way in. "Ahhhh!" I cried out. I'd tried to ride him dry like this once before, and I was brutally sore for two days. But I was too famished to sweat it. I started working him up and down. After a few minutes of that, my hands braced on his shoulders. Soon I could ride him harder; those nasty plunging noises his dick makes inside me were filling the room.

But I couldn't ride him as hard as I needed. On the up stroke, I grasped upward. My hand slapped a chest-pull workout handle Jackson had drilled to the ceiling.

I had an idea …. "Hang on!" I said, lifting off his cock with a slurp. I grabbed the other chest grip with my left hand. With one in each, I could brace myself and pull down.

"Put it in me!" I told him. Jackson guided his tip inside me and I started riding. It took me some thrusts to figure out how far I could pull on those grips and then raise myself back up. Soon you could hear the whooshing noise as I got the hang of the pull. Before long I was riding him like crazy, pounding his cock inside me as if it could bludgeon all my doubts.

I was actually scared. If I pulled all the way out thrusting this hard, I would slam back down on Jackson, hurting him if not myself. Jackson grabbed me at the tip and pulled me down to keep the thrusts going.

"Fuck me!" I screamed, though I was really fucking *him*. I could feel an epic cum welling up inside of me, if we could just keep thrusting ….

"Oh my god!" I screamed. I had forgotten how badly I needed to cum. It was as if that botched scene with Alicia had lit a sexual time bomb inside my body. I put my anger at Jackson out of my mind and rode him for all I could, right through one orgasm and onto the next. But the tsunami cum hadn't hit yet.

Jackson knew my body so well by now; he could tell I was going to have a mega cum. That's what Jackson and I called it—a mega cum, or crazy cum. It was the type of cum a girl can have on a skilled lover with a big cock, where your whole pussy is turned inside out from the rhythm, and your entire body gets caught up in the spasms. Twenty or thirty times more intense than a clit orgasm, a mega cum is an itch that starts deep inside and then lights a fuse, and then … fucking look out! I've even (briefly) passed out from a cum like that. Many times, I've cried tears of physical and emotional joy.

"You're going to cum crazy!" he said, holding me on his dick so I wouldn't pop out. Sure enough, my thighs started shaking, like an erotic seizure was ripping through me.

"Oh … my … god." I dropped into Jackson's arms. The intensity of that cum was just what I needed. For the next minute or so, my legs trembled on top of him as my entire body exhaled. God, he played my body like a fucking Stradivarius.

If you're thinking this encounter led to our reconciliation, you'd be wrong. I was not willing to let Jackson win my heart back through orgasms. I have far too much pride for that. Jackson did seem kind of smug the next few days as we went about our business. But he accepted the boundaries of our intimacy.

Jackson isn't book smart, but when it comes to women, he is one wily coyote. That motherfucker knew if he just let me thaw out at room temperature, eventually there would be an opening.

After about six weeks of garage living, the dam broke. It was a Friday night. Chelsea was at a slumber party. Jackson and I ended up watching a movie in the living room together—*Fury Road*, I think.

It was nothing pre-planned, but we each had a Guinness. Well, maybe I had two. And it was relaxing just to be around him, without him begging to take me back. Just movie banter. But alcohol is my truth serum, so after a while, I hit "pause" on the movie, and cut to the chase.

"Was she the first?"

He knew exactly what I meant. "You want the truth?" he said.

"Out with it," I said, pulling my legs back to my chest in a defensive position.

"Yes, she was the first. Since our marriage, she was the first."

I felt relief, I'm not sure why, given how easily he could be lying.

"But—"

Uh oh.

"It wasn't the first time with her."

WTF?

"It started a year ago. She made me some lemonade …"

Lemonade? What a cliché! You have got to be kidding me.

"And ended up sucking my dick," he finished, too smugly for my taste.

"She was desperate for it; it was hard to resist."

"Oh no you didn't!" The way I said it made Jackson crack a smile, but I wasn't buying it.

"Oh yes I did," he said, acting the fool. "But look at it this way—I've never been faithful for six months before, much less eight years."

God, I hated that kind of excuse. But then Jackson turned on me. With a glare he said, "I've had a lot of time to think in that garage about how I ended up there. I warned you about this before we married. I'm not sure I can stay faithful, and frankly, I don't intend to anymore."

It was a kick in the damn gut. But I was going to finish the argument.

"And why is that?"

"You want the truth?"

"Yes, I want the fucking truth, Jackson!"

"Okay, here goes …" and Jackson looked me straight in the eye and said one of the most absurd things I've ever heard come out of a man's mouth, "I believe I was brought on this earth to make women feel amazing. It's the thing I'm best at. And I've decided that I'm not going to let anyone—including you," he said for emphasis, "get in the way of that any longer."

"Are you fucking kidding me, Jackson? That is *the most* ridiculous thing I have ever heard."

I didn't know whether to laugh or slap his egocentric face.

So … I slapped him. It felt good, and it was hard enough to leave a big red splotch.

I reached out to smack him again but Jackson grabbed my arm and patiently guided it to my side.

That gave me pause, and I fell back into contemplation. More questions:

"So why the hell was Brad in the room?"

"Well, he started watching us … at the suggestion of Alicia."

"What do you mean he 'started watching'? He's done this more than once with you?"

"Oh yeah," Jackson said with a weird grin. "I lost count at ten."

"Why does he watch?"

"Well, he likes to experience the intensity of watching another man fuck his wife."

Sounded fucking nuts.

"And he doesn't want to deny her what I can give her any longer," Jackson said, forcefully, *confidently*. I wanted to smack his goddamn face again. Almost did.

"I find it hard to believe he can't make his own wife happy," I said. "Why would they be married then?"

"Well, the attraction faded … for her anyway," Jackson said. "But they still want a life together. And she doesn't want to cheat."

I had no words.

"You must have seen … how small his cock was," Jackson said.

I didn't really remember, though I did have an image of his hand moving up and down—not so much his dick, but his hand.

"Not really …" I said. Now, I would never have admitted it then, but I can't deny it now: this was the first time I started to feel a slight tingle at the frankness of this conversation.

"Well, she had never cum from penetration during her marriage."

"I took care of that the first time I was with her," Jackson continued. Now he was grinning from ear to ear, without a trace of the guilt I was expecting out of that cheating son-of-a-bitch.

"She was … pretty darn grateful," he added. "Eventually, he was too."

"He was … grateful?" This defied explanation.

"Oh yeah," Jackson said. "He knew Alicia had been cheating on him now and then. He always wondered if it was because of his own, well, inadequacies. It ate at him.

"Now he knows the answer to that question," Jackson continued. "And … she doesn't cheat on him anymore. It's all out in the open." Jackson paused, then added, "They told me how much closer they are emotionally. No more secrets, no more hiding." Jackson was speaking with a gangsta Dr. Phil seriousness. As if I would buy into this whole mess as a mental health exercise!

"Well good for them, and good for you!" I said, storming out of the room.

"Garage?" Jackson asked expectantly.

"Yes!" I yelled without looking back.

For a while, I couldn't sleep at all. But then my anger at Jackson gave way to a realization: *I know what I have to do.*

Chapter 7

THE NEXT MORNING, I called in one of my rare sick days. My secretary Lizzy was genuinely concerned. I'm never sick, and now I had used two sick days in seven weeks.

"Lizzy," I confided, "I'm not really sick. I just have … something I need to take care of."

Lizzy had met Jackson before. "Well, okay …" was all she said, but her conspiratorial subtext said, "Hot husbands bring problems, but they are worth it." As long as Lizzy could cover for me, I didn't care.

I washed my hair carefully, deliberately. Shaved my legs and even plucked a couple of stray eyebrows—the kind of stuff I might do before a big business meeting. But I wasn't going to meet a new client.

An hour later, I was knocking on Alicia's door. I could see her eyes flash through the peephole. Then, a good long hesitation.

"Don't worry, Alicia, I'm unarmed!"

More silence. Perhaps the anger in my voice was less than reassuring.

Alicia cautiously pried open the door, sticking her angular face out. I wanted to punch it.

"Yes?"

"I think you know why I'm here."

The door shut.

But then the chain rattled. Alicia opened the door deliberately, assessing my threat level.

"Corrie, please come in."

I barged in, trying to still my quivering knees. My memories of the next few minutes are hazy. I know Alicia brought me into the kitchen. I remember her pouring some kind of hard alcohol into a blender full of frozen strawberries. I remember the whirring sound as she whipped up our drinks, awkwardly postponing our conversation.

I stared longingly at the knife rack mounted on the cupboard—Was Jackson responsible for that handiwork?—thinking how easy it would be to simply pull a knife out and ….

I remember Alicia pouring frozen drinks into two glass juicing jars and leading me to the back porch.

The glare was fierce. I sucked down half that drink without saying a thing as the sun beat down.

Alicia didn't say anything either. She let me sit, bake, and suck through an straw. Clever little slut ….

As much as I hate to admit it, with the sun baking the porch and the drink in my veins, I started feeling kind of, well … relaxed. No. Somehow I felt *good*.

As if my life wasn't falling apart, or as if my marriage wasn't ruptured. Somehow, some way, everything was going to be okay. God, that's a wonderful feeling when it sneaks up on you. And it can sneak up at the unlikeliest of times.

I had never thought of Alicia as an attractive woman the way my drooling guy friends did. Maybe she wasn't my type; I wasn't crazy about her boyish hairstyle. But, stealing glances as the sun steamed the pavement, I couldn't help but notice that her body seemed strong and supple. And she was pretty damn relaxed in it. She had some ass-hugging denim shorts on, and a T-shirt cut low.

Alicia hadn't bothered to comb her short blonde hair. I tried to tell myself she was too masculine-looking for Jackson. But there was something about her. Like the way she didn't rush into some big apology, or for that matter, say anything at all.

There was only one thing left to say. I had only one reason to be here. I finally found the words: "Why?"

"Well, this is pretty personal," Alicia said.

"I'd say fucking my husband is pretty personal also."

"Okay," she exhaled, and then said, "Are you familiar with the word 'cuckold'?"

"You mean, like a woman who cheats on her husband?"

"Well, yeah, but that's not really what I mean." Alicia hesitated for a moment. "You see …." She sat up straight in her wicker chair. Maybe she sensed I needed the short version: "My husband is a cuckold. We didn't start out that way. We were head over heels in love. He was my everything," her eyes were wistful, "but a few years into our marriage, I started to get, well, bored.

"We tried a few things, to spice things up—toys, date nights, lingerie—but then we met a couple who was into swapping. We decided to try it. It wasn't great at first, but after I got another man inside me, there wasn't any going back."

I noticed she had skipped the cheating part Jackson had told me about.

"Suddenly I knew. If I was going to stay in this marriage, we would need something like this."

Alicia seemed to be drawing comfort from confessing. I wasn't crazy about the comfort part.

"Brad liked the swinging, too, but after a few times, we figured out he actually liked to watch *me* have sex more than he liked making love to someone else." She sighed. "And that's what makes him a cuckold—the way we talk about it."

"And Jackson?" I brought Alicia back to the point.

"Well, I really regret it."

My eyes narrowed.

"Jackson was sure you couldn't handle it. He said that you would be really, really pissed off if you ever found out … and he was right. I didn't like the feeling that I was betraying you, Corrie. But the sex was just … well, you know." She gave me a knowing glance. I hate to admit that I felt an immediate bond with her. *I did know.* It would have been so very easy to reach over and smack some pink into her face.

"And so I couldn't really help myself," she continued. "I found all kinds of ways to rationalize it. But I think in the end, it was just something that felt really fucking good. I was just so sexually famished, and Jackson, well, he …."

It was the first really honest thing to come out of her mouth. But it was a start. We had a bit of history, and I suppose that helped us. But we weren't there yet.

I commanded Alicia to make us another round of drinks. That's one good thing about being cheated on—you can be *very* demanding.

While she made the drinks, my brain cooked in the sun while I tried to make sense of it all. I didn't have any experiences that connected to this, even remotely.

Well, except for your fiancé, Daniel.

Yeah, except for that. Damn that thought! Shame and remorse ripped through me. Daniel would have never put me in this situation. Sweet Daniel. A horrid thought snuck in:

Maybe you aren't so innocent. Maybe you're quite a bit like Alicia.

Flush that!

When she came back, I came at her hard. Verbally, that is.

"Alicia, I'm going to need more from you. You fucked my fucking husband."

"I'll tell you anything you want to know." When she said it, she crossed her legs in a way that emphasized their musculature. If I hadn't known better, I'd have thought she was trying to make a sexual impression on me. Well, I was not in the mood.

"Alicia, every marriage hits the wall from time to time. Just being bored isn't a good reason to fuck whomever you choose."

"Well, like I said, I didn't fuck whomever I chose," Alicia responded, "not until Jackson, anyhow." Another attempt at a conspiratorial, sisterly grin.

I wasn't having any of it. "But there are classes, therapists. Share your fantasies, work on your lovemaking skills. You don't need someone else's husband when you have each other."

"That's easy for you to say," Alicia said.

"How so?"

"You're married to one of the best fucks on the planet."

"Well, if you're in love with someone, you love them as they are. You ... make love to them."

"Yeah, well, that works ... sometimes. But Brad has, well, shortcomings where Jackson doesn't. And there isn't a class for that."

"What do you mean?" I knew exactly what she meant, but after what she put me through, I was going to make her say it.

"My husband has a small dick." She smiled at me. It wasn't hard for her to say after all.

"So what?" I asked. "How is that my problem?"

"Well ... Jackson, he can fuck so much better. It just feels so good and he, well, he makes me do things and say things and feel things my husband just can't."

I was offended, but I respected her bluntness.

"But here's the thing, Alicia: you shouldn't have married him in the first place. If he couldn't satisfy you, you should never have taken vows. You were just a slutty time bomb waiting to go off on someone's husband!"

She snorted. "Well, I didn't know that at the time. Besides, I was in love."

By now we were almost shouting at each other.

"You mean, you don't know what a small penis is?" I mocked her.

"Well I do now, but I didn't then."

"Why not?"

"Because I had never been fucked properly!" Alicia yelled. "Not until after I was married," she continued more calmly.

"Ah, so you're a slut then."

"I'm not a slut. I just … have my needs."

"So you did what?"

"Well, a couple years into my marriage, I ended up fucking my massage therapist."

"And?"

"He gave me the first vaginal orgasm of my life … and then a lot more of them."

"See? You're a slut!" It was a pleasure saying it to her face, even if I wasn't sure I believed it. Or if she was, then so was I. *Fuck her!*

"Maybe. No. I don't know. All I know is that pretty soon after my wedding, I was plagued by feelings of intense attraction for men not my husband." She shook her head. "For a while, I ignored those feelings, I really did. I tried like hell to make my marriage work—in the bedroom, outside the bedroom. I found myself wondering if I had married too young, or married the wrong man. Or yeah, if I was … well, a slut."

For a moment I forgot about Jackson and had a few moments of empathy for Alicia. *Daniel!*

"In the beginning, it didn't occur to me that my husband wasn't physically able to satisfy me," said Alicia. "But it wasn't just that. I guess, deep down, I had some unspeakable desire … a desire to be taken—just fucking taken! And my husband … well, I adore him, but he has never *taken* me."

I stopped asking angry questions. *That is exactly what happened with Daniel and Jackson.*

Not that I was going to tell her anything about that. Between my legs I felt signs of life.

"The guys I was attracted to after I married … they were guys with raw confidence."

"The massage therapist?" I prompted, wanting Alicia to jump ahead.

"Yeah … the massage therapist. I was so damned attracted to him." Alicia sighed. "I didn't even know he had a big manly cock that made my husband's look like a little schoolboy's." She laughed.

I found myself laughing too. "But you found out," I prompted.

"Oh yeah, I found out many, many times," Alicia said. More laughter from both of us. "He really filled me up with his big penis, and he knew just how to work it. He was the first man who … could really make me feel like a woman. Really take over my body. Well, you know."

I do. Goddamn it, Alicia, I do.

"As good as Jackson?"

"Not as good as Jackson. Oh no," Alicia insisted.

We exchanged another smile, and for a moment I felt a swirling, ludicrous pride. I quickly put on my serious face. I wasn't here for giggly girl talk, damn it! Nevertheless, I felt another tingling sensation, this time extending through my hips and up to my nipples.

"But your massage therapist?" I pressed.

"Yes," said Alicia. "And the weirdest thing is I didn't even have a crush on him. I actually had a crush on his business partner, Bruce, who was built like a brick shithouse. This guy, Oregon, was hippie-dippie; he'd wear these tie-dye T-shirts and yoga pants. I only tried him because Bruce had the flu. Turned out this wiry dude gave better massages than Bruce. It was like he knew my body better and the points to push. And well, I guess my body turned him on because a few times I thought I saw his crotch bulge out a bit. It looked really big, but I told myself it was just fabric," Alicia said.

I crossed and uncrossed my legs, feeling the effects of the story.

"I started coming in every week," Alicia said, "but I made up a reason to come in on Bruce's day off. And the baggy pants and hippie-dippie vibe didn't bother me anymore. I started looking forward to his hands on my body." She smiled. "Then, one week, I asked him to spend some extra time on my lower back, knowing he'd be near my ass. I made a point of lifting my ass in the air in response to his touch. Then I closed my eyes as if I was falling asleep. Anyhow, I opened my eyes a few minutes later and was shocked to see his big thick penis poking right out of his fly. I guess he liked to air it out sometimes when I was napping."

"And …?"

"I gasped, and we had an awkward moment. I insisted that he had to let me hold it if he wanted to stay out of trouble." Alicia giggled.

"Just a little blackmail, huh?"

"Well, I just had to touch it and hold it. Once I held it, I had to ask him questions about it. It was just so much bigger than Brad's." She knew she was getting me hot. "Anyhow," she went on, "while I stroked him, I asked Oregon—yes, that was really his birth name—about his sexual history."

"Why?"

"Well, I knew a lot about Brad's history and basic lack of sexual experience. He'd had only three sexual partners before me. I wondered how different Oregon's experience was. He seemed so confident with this body."

"And …" I said. This discussion was turning so hot that I had to mentally forbid my right hand not to rub my pussy under the table.

"Well, it was hard to get the truth, because Oregon didn't want me to think he was just a male slut," she said, "but I finally got him to admit he had fucked well over fifty women, and at twenty-five, he was only a year older than Brad."

"Wow!" I said.

"He lost his virginity seven years earlier that Brad. So, anyhow, I flat out asked him if he thought his big penis was the reason he got laid so much." She paused, seeing how I hung on her every word. "He basically said yes," she finally continued. "He said that he got a lot of word-of-mouth referrals. He liked that girls initially thought he was this weird hippie. He'd fuck the hell out of one of their friends, and then the whole way they looked at him changed." Her eyes grew wide. "He told me that he had fucked—get this—*five* of his brother's girlfriends. Turns out Oregon got all the dick in his family and his older brother got none."

"Oh my god!" I said. By now I was rubbing myself under the table. I couldn't help it. I'm pretty sure Alicia could tell, but I'll bet she preferred me horny over angry. "Wasn't his brother pissed?"

"I asked him about that," Oregon said. "His brother was really mad at first, but the second girl Oregon fucked threatened to tell the whole school he had a tiny penis if he said anything about her fucking Oregon." She leaned forward and touched my arm. "Then, get this … she made him stand next to his brother and stroke his tiny dick while she worked Oregon's big one."

"Oh my fucking god," I said. Jesus, this was getting crazier and hotter.

"And then she made him watch while Oregon fucked her brains out, humiliating him the whole time."

I was speechless.

"After that, I guess Oregon's older brother developed a fetish for bringing his girlfriends home and getting Oregon to seduce them, or arranging for them to see Oregon naked and see what would happen and if they were interested." Alicia shook her head. "Well, needless to say, that gave me plenty of ideas for my own marriage."

"So you just jacked him off for hours while getting his sexual life history," I said, trying to distract myself from my intense need to masturbate.

"Ha ha! Not exactly. I got about twenty minutes of history out of him before our appointment was about to end. I did want to see him cum and it was a sight to behold."

"Messy?"

"Oh yeah ..." Alicia said. "The hottest part was knowing, with one hundred percent absolute certainty, that his big cock was going to be filling my pussy someday."

God, I felt a huge jolt in my pussy when she said that.

"Of course I didn't even know if it would fit. But he assured me that it would. Told me only two girls had trouble with it and they were both virgins. He said 'I just need to get you warmed up right, and it will feel sooo good.' "

"And ...?"

"And he was fucking right! I'm not sure if I'd ever cum on Brad's cock. I thought I had, but after I came all over Oregon, I reconsidered."

We both paused, lost in our own sexual memories, I suppose.

"Sometimes I think I need to write Susie a thank you note."

"Susie?" I asked.

"Susie was the mother of one of his friends—the hottest mother around, or so he said. He credited Susie with teaching him how to use his big penis, how to warm girls up first, which positions to use, and how to last inside a woman."

"Jackson had an older teacher too," I couldn't help confiding.

"Now why doesn't that surprise me?" Alicia asked. "Anyhow, Oregon said once he got those tutorials from Susie, his success rate with women his own age shot through the roof. Before, they were curious. Now they were addicted."

I was having a hard time keeping myself under control. Thinking about Oregon fucking his older brother's girlfriends was so hot for some reason. I was distracted from my purpose. I excused myself to go to the bathroom, and once inside, promptly got my fingers into my grateful pussy.

Sticking my fingers into my panties in a strange woman's bathroom made me feel so fucking naughty that my knees buckled. I worked my pussy feverishly with my right hand, bracing against the door by gripping the towel rack with my left. I came while leaning against the bathroom door, rubbing my clit until it moved from "scratch that itch" to the unbearable lightness of cumming. As I spasmed, I pulled so hard on the towel rack, a screw popped loose. I was *that* close to knocking the whole thing down on my head.

I pushed the screw back inside the rack and shimmied back into my panties. That rack could be Alicia's problem another day.

When I came back, Alicia had a sneaky look on her face. If she knew what I was up to, she was courteous enough to keep it to herself.

"So … did you fuck Oregon in front of Brad?"

"No. I tried to work that out, but Oregon didn't want to do that anymore. I think a part of him wanted to move on from the person he was back then, fucking his brother's girls. I tried to tell him this would be different, that Brad wouldn't mind, but I never could talk him into it. Back then, I hadn't talked to Brad about this, but I was willing to do almost anything to keep that sex going." She sighed, then continued, "Not too long after, Oregon got engaged to a very possessive yoga bitch." When I laughed, she grinned. "Still," she went on, "the damage was done."

"Damage?"

"That's when I realized that I had married someone who was inadequate for me sexually, and that … well … our marriage was in trouble."

We were silent for a moment, letting that sober thought sink in.

"But you kept cheating on Brad, didn't you?"

"Yeah. And you know what? I didn't feel the slightest bit guilty about it."

"You didn't? God, you are such a bitch!"

"Well, I did feel guilty … for the married women, or the girlfriends. It seemed like every guy I wanted to fuck, or who could fuck me the way I wanted, had a serious girlfriend."

"Funny how that works," I said pointedly.

Alicia flushed. "I lived in fear that I would be caught. Maybe a part of me wanted to be. Just blow my whole damn life up, go back to being a broke bar chick. But thank god, it never came to that."

"I guess not," I said, resisting a move for the jugular. I wanted to know this part of the story. "So, what changed?"

"Well, one night Brad made me a really nice dinner at home. And then he told me something I'll never forget. He said, 'I think I'm a cuckold.' I thought he was accusing me of cheating on him, and a stake went through my heart." She pounded her chest for emphasis. But then she shrugged. "He had known about the cheating for a while. He had even read some of my text messages. Honestly, I don't think I was too careful." She met my eyes. "I was scared shitless. I figured Brad would dump me on the spot. But when Brad said 'cuckold,' he didn't mean being cheated on. What he meant was that his place in our relationship was to be, well, submissive to me and my lovers."

"What?" I said, incredulous.

"Yeah, he said he knew he couldn't satisfy me sexually. He understood why I cheated on him, or at least he thought he understood. He said he needed to watch me fuck to make sure. I couldn't believe Brad said that to me, and it took me some days to wrap my brain around it. I really did love him. And I realized this might give us a chance to save our marriage. And of course, I remembered what Oregon said. I'll never forget it, because he wasn't just referring to his brother. He said some men love the humiliation and intensity of seeing their girlfriends fucked right in front of them. He'd had a college roommate who was into it."

"So what happened?" I prodded.

"Well, Brad did watch me fuck."

"With who?" I figured she would say "Jackson," and felt my fists clench.

"I was fucking the Cyclops then."

"The Cyclops?"

"That was the nickname I gave this guy from CrossFit. He

only had one ball, but he had one heck of a dick!"

Once we stopped laughing, Alicia continued, "Yeah, so, my husband watched the Cyclops fuck me, and even though it wasn't his best outing, I did cum all over his penis a few times, which made a big impression on Brad. After the Cyclops left, I forced my Brad to fuck me. I couldn't feel his tiny dick at all."

"And …?"

"Well, it was really hard for him … humiliating even. But Brad squirted inside my pussy while he thrust like a rabbit."

More laughter. We women can be so cruel.

"Anyhow," Alicia sighed, "it wasn't easy on either side, but we came to an agreement. He told me I could no longer cheat on him, now that everything was out in the open."

"Holy shit. What did you say?"

"I almost told him he could go stroke his little dick off to his heart's content, because I was going to fuck whoever I wanted from now on … whether I told him about it or not. But then I gave it some real hard thought, and I realized I could live with his requirement. Truth be told, I probably needed his pushback. I was a bit out of control. If he hadn't demanded some accountability from me, I would have seen him as weak outside the bedroom also … so weak I probably would have left him. And you know what?" Alicia said, raising her eyebrows. "I respected him for it. For taking a stand. For granting me freedom but imposing a limit."

"But that doesn't get us to here." With my orgasm behind me, I was all business.

"Well, I still told him that I could fuck anyone I wanted, and that he could stroke his tiny dick off if he didn't like it. I'm not sure if I could have stopped if he asked me. I've always wondered that. But he didn't ask me to stop."

"How can you have any trust, living like this?"

"Talk, talk, talk," Alicia said, "and no cheating. No shortcuts. I told him I would never do it behind his back, and he could always choose to be involved. It's been five years since then."

Alicia paused. "At first, Corrie, he did wonder if he could trust me. Then he saw that as long as I was getting what I needed, I had nothing to hide. Things … well, they changed for the better. I'm sure we'd be divorced by now otherwise."

Alicia had thrown me. I'm not a little-pink-houses woman, but her relationship was well out of my comfort zone.

"Don't get me wrong," Alicia hurried to add. "Things have definitely changed in our relationship … especially in the bedroom. I guess we both had to let go of something there. But we're closer than ever. All my married friends would say that. So, something is working."

"So, what exactly has changed, other than the obvious?" I said. I felt like she owed me the story behind the story.

"Well, Brad and I still fool around a lot, but it's almost like we're back in high school or something."

"High school?"

"Yeah. You remember those early dates where you weren't ready to fuck, so you kind of fooled around—"

"Yes," I said, kind of lying. I pretty much went straight from innocent kissing to fucking. But most of my girlfriends had taken their time, so I got Alicia's drift.

"Well, with Brad, we don't fuck that much anymore. His penis is just too small for me now. Damn, I'm spoiled, I guess! I can barely feel him anymore, and I get impatient when he's inside me. But he can still eat me like a champ, and we have a lot of fun just, well, being close. We really don't have any secrets between us, and that is an amazing feeling in its own right. I guess it's like high school in that regard too—we got a bit of that 'first love' feeling back between us."

We both paused to let that revelation soak in. Then Alicia sat up in her chair and said, "But here's the strange thing: I was submitting so completely to my lovers, but I also realized that I had a dominant side, and I unleashed it on Brad more in the bedroom. He opened up to a submissive side that shamed him but that he also craved to experience."

"Craved?" I asked.

"Brad loves to be teased and humiliated for his sexual inadequacies," said Alicia. "And to be honest, I love to do it. I think past experiences I had with arrogant, small-dicked men add to the intensity of what I dish out to him. It's kind of cathartic to finally let a small-dicked guy know just how disappointing he is. But I do worry I am dumping my past frustrations on him."

"Like you're getting revenge on other guys who couldn't fuck you, and who tried to control you in other ways," I theorized.

"Yes, something like that," Alicia said. "Looking back, I hate the time I wasted with overcompensating jerks. Maybe this gives me some outlet for that." After a moment of thought, she said, "Fortunately, Brad's little dick likes it."

"What do you mean?" I asked her.

"Well, he gets so hard when I tease him about his inadequacy …. His little dick squirts in my hand and he's like putty for the rest of the day."

I didn't really understand but I laughed with Alicia anyway.

"I never …" I began.

"You never what?" asked Alicia.

"I guess I never realized … that small guys would get off on that. I was usually too busy rejecting them—either in subtle ways or outright." My mind flashed on Daniel—how kind he was. How angry he'd been on the phone the last time we talked. *Ugh*.

I waited in silence while Alicia fetched ice and beverage refills. When she sat back down, she said, "The weird thing is, while I'm very dominant in bed with Brad, I'm totally submissive with my bulls."

"Bulls?" I asked.

Alicia laughed. "Oh yeah, I didn't tell you. In cuckolding circles, guys like Jackson are referred to as bulls."

My husband *the bull*? WTH?

"And what defines a bull?"

"Well, each women might think of it differently. But a bull is usually naturally dominant, used to taking control and easily making us submit to him. But I have my own view on that," Alicia went on. "For me, a bull can simply fuck a lot better than Brad. Usually he has a much bigger cock, and he can literally rip the orgasms from my body, even if I'm initially not really in the mood for sex. Whereas with Brad, I have to be in a certain mood emotionally to even want to spread for him." Her eyes widened. "A bull like Jackson, though, he can get me wet and make me cum no matter how pissed off I am, no matter how much I don't want to submit to him in that moment."

The "bull" part of this language was super-weird, but I must admit I was very familiar with the bull part of things with men, and that feeling of surrendering to ecstasy. I guess I understood that more. But Brad?

"Oh, and I'd say Brad and I are more like best friends than intense sexual partners."

"What do you mean?" I asked.

Alicia paused, then continued, "Well, I can't say that I ever get weak in the knees around him the way I did when we first met." She shrugged. "I guess you could say I have a lot of power in the relationship. And that kind of changes my attraction to him." She waggled her forefinger. "But not *all* the power, because I'm pretty sure he would leave me for good if I cheated on him. And … well, I think it's good for me that I don't have absolute power in this. I would not only run him into the ground; I'd lose myself."

I had to spit it out: "But … you're still hurting other women—the wives and girlfriends of the other men you've fucked!" The time for reflection was over; I wanted my pound of flesh.

Alicia looked like she'd been punched. Finally she said, "I know. Corrie, I'm really sorry. I won't … fuck Jackson again. I promise."

For a second, I thought I saw a tear in Alicia's eye. She didn't have to say anything more. I recognized it from that summer with Daniel and Jackson. I had felt conflicted, out of control, unable to get a handle on my own passions. Is that the way all women are? Or can be?

No matter. I wasn't giving Alicia that excuse. Or that comfort. I got up quickly, before my resolve faded.

"Okay, Alicia," I said, "I'm going to hold you to that." And that was all the understanding I was ready to give her.

I scooted off the chair, back through her house and out, before she could say anything more or even close the door behind me. I gave it a good slam.

I made a point of pressing the accelerator in my Mustang, leaving Alicia some road burn.

Chapter 8

ONCE HOME, I WAS able to put the masturbation incident and its implications behind me. Alicia had agreed to never fuck Jackson again, and I believed her. If I asked Jackson, he would say the same. So … one problem solved. But what about other women?

If I ask Jackson not to fuck any other women, will he agree?

Deep down—and damn it, this is humiliating—I wasn't sure if he was willing to stop. Not even for me—the queen, the damn princess, the girl with the most cake. A part of me wanted to force the matter to a head, compelling him to make a choice. But as much as I hated it—as much as it drove me bonkers—a primal part of me loved that he had the sexual upper hand. No other man could make that claim. Please don't think less of me for this, but you could say it made my pussy sopping wet. And this:

Daniel would never have given you that type of ultimatum.

It was a terrible, horrible, no good thought—and one hundred percent true. If you think it made Daniel look good in my mind, actually, it was the opposite. It made me respect him less. No, not *respect* exactly … desire. It made me want Daniel less. Maybe that's fucked up, I don't know.

And: *Jackson is a perfect sex partner. Because you can't control him. He won't let you.*

But then, the burning question: how do you make a life with someone like that?

At home in the shower, washing the cum Alicia had provoked off my thighs, I couldn't stop the fierce debate between my own thought demons:

Monogamy is easier for Daniel than Jackson. Women are throwing themselves at Jackson all the time. Asking a man who fucks that well to keep it in his pants, was that realistic?

Well, I don't give a fuck about realistic!

And there, left leg propped up on a bath stool, I teased myself off again, imagining all the hot women Jackson had fucked. Alicia was the tip of that particular iceberg. I swear, women can sense how good Jackson can make them feel.

Yikes.

AFTER THAT, I DIDN'T masturbate again. Not that week, not the next. Nor did I fuck Jackson again. He was around the house here and there, spending time with Chelsea, sleeping in the garage. Sometimes, after I fell asleep, he'd grab a blanket and head for the living room couch. That was all I let him get away with. A couple times, he made his moves on me, but I resisted. It was as if all the sex had been drained from my body.

One night during that celibate period, I had a rough dream. After waking up with a start, I checked the couch, but Jackson was missing. I stormed out to the garage, sure he was gone, but no … he was curled up on the creaky fold-out, snoring on his back.

I asked him to come back to bed. I just needed to feel his strong arms around me. I slept without worries.

In the morning, I knew what I had to do.

"Jackson!" I woke him rudely, tapping on his arm, a full hour before his alarm. He was going to have a sleepy day on the job.

"Yeah?"

He propped himself up, rubbing the sleep from his eyes.

"You said that Alicia's husband watched you fuck."

"Yeah. But why does that matter now?"

"Because … if he watched, I want to watch too."

"What do you mean?"

"I want to see what he saw. I want to see his reactions. I want to be there."

Jackson hesitated, confused. I think he'd expected me to discuss our future, not propose a sex tryst. And my proposal would hardly bring closure to our problems; it would open up another big-ass can of worms.

"I don't know if that's a good idea," he protested.

"I don't care! Set it up."

And with that, I hit the shower.

I knew that eventually they would all agree. Alicia and Jackson didn't really have a choice. And as for Alicia's husband … if what they said about him was true, well, he would welcome such a crazy situation.

A week later, it was all set. Misgivings had been expressed on all sides, but I think Jackson understood what was at stake.

So we found ourselves once again sitting awkwardly on Alicia's back porch, this time together. I was casually dressed in hip-hugging jeans and a blouse far too generic for such a taboo occasion. Alicia was wearing overalls under a bulky shirt, as if pretending this wasn't happening. Jackson, busting out of his T-shirt and cargos, was the only one who looked the part.

Brad, meanwhile, was the odd man out. He wore a T-shirt as well and Docker shorts, but his clothes fit awkwardly, as if hanging from a bent clothes hanger. Brad forced a smile, but he couldn't carry us through our casual, forced conversation. I think we actually talked about the weather. Then, sports. *Yawn*.

Brad seemed proud of having more stats at his mental disposal than Jackson. That's about all I recall from that draggy conversation. I figured some loosening up might be in order, so in my purse I had compassionately stashed a small joint, procured for this occasion. Smoking helped a little. I suppose this was not like swinging, where two couples look forward to coming events with the same anticipation. This time, everyone was accommodating me.

Alicia tried to break the tension. "Let me get us … another round of …" and she escaped to the kitchen.

But somehow, I knew what to do.

"Alicia, that won't be necessary," I called after her. "Why don't you and Jackson head to the bedroom while Brad and I have a chat."

Alicia's conflicted expression relaxed into relief. At least she knew how to play this particular part. She and Jackson headed inside after exchanging a knowing look that annoyed me no end. That left me to the awkwardness of Brad.

Things got even more bizarre. Brad wasn't what you would call a chillaxed stoner. He seemed twitchy. Settling into my chair, I sipped my cocktail as if Brad and I were old pals. I was starting to enjoy his predicament.

Brad was fed up.

"Why … w-why are you doing this?" he stammered.

"Well, Brad, you like to watch. What gives you the right to watch and not me?"

"But … this is what me and my wife do. You're here … just because you're mad."

"Well, yeah, I'm pissed!" I said. "You guys kept something pretty damn important from me."

"Jackson kept you out of this because he was afraid how you'd respond," Brad blurted out. "Like this!" he added.

I was kind of impressed by Brad. Yeah, his anger had a desperate quality, but he wasn't the pushover I had expected.

"Okay, Brad, let me explain. When my spouse does something I don't approve of, there are consequences. Or does that word not have relevance for you?"

Brad's face flushed. Time for me to get my blows in.

"I don't let the men I fuck just put their dicks wherever they want, much less my husband," I continued. "Not like Alicia, who spreads her legs whether you fucking like it or not."

Hurt flashed across Brad's face. "I'm just … I'm just trying to keep my marriage alive. I don't … I don't want to lose Alicia. I'm … well, I'm afraid. Afraid of where this could lead. I'm not … comfortable with her feelings for Jackson."

"Well, that makes two of us!" I snapped.

"And for what it's worth," he continued, "I'm sorry."

In spite of myself, I empathized with him. We were both trying to hang on to what was ours, or what we thought of as ours.

Now I was distracted, but for a different reason. Something I had not expected.

I clutched Brad's hand. He did not pull away.

"Brad, I'll be dead honest with you," I said. "I don't know why I'm here either. Like you said, it was more … an emotional reaction. Like you, I'm trying to save my marriage, in my own fucked-up way."

We both chuckled at the absurdity of that.

"But," I paused, looking for words, "I'm starting to think there might be something here for me too. Something very, very bad."

I thought I saw a twitch in Brad's pants. I flashed to my furious masturbation session after the last time at Alicia's. But I didn't tell him about that.

"Brad, I think what we need to do is watch what is happening in that bedroom."

We locked eyes. I'm not sure if he was excited, or terrified, or both.

"I can't tell you what's going to happen, Brad. I've never been down this road before. But I know I need to see this, and … I need you to be here too."

Brad seemed surprised.

"Why … me?"

"Brad, I'm not sure. I really need to find out."

Then I stood up, still holding his hand. I was almost towering over him now. Then I went for the jugular, "Brad, don't you need to know too?"

He didn't have to say anything. His face was a yes.

I took Brad's hand and led him toward the bedroom.

"Wow, just follow the moans," I laughed as we got near.

When I opened the door, it was just about the perfect moment.

Alicia, already buck naked, was kneeling on the floor. She was cautiously pulling Jackson's boxers down, as if afraid of what she might find there.

Jackson's cock popped out, just as it had for me so many times, maybe two thirds hard, bonking Alicia in the face before landing proudly in her hands.

Slutty hands, I thought to myself.

Alicia and Jackson looked over at us, but I didn't want them to stop.

"Keep going, Alicia!" I said. "I want to see how you work it."

Alicia blushed, but she was too far gone to stop.

Letting go of my hand, Brad went into the walk-in closet and dragged out a large sofa chair.

"I see you prepared for this, Brad," I whispered into his ear. Blushing, he asked me if I wanted a folding chair.

"No, Brad, I think we can share this one."

Brad had set up the chair about eight feet from the bed, and he sat down to watch the action. I stood behind him, leaning over as Alicia starting working Jackson's penis.

The sight made me a little sick. But it also sent a jolt down my body and between my legs. I braced the chair for support.

Here we go. I thought. *Here we go.*

I leaned over and whispered into Brad's ear, possessed by some strange new purpose.

"Look at her, Brad. She's already lost it."

Brad moaned and started rubbing himself through his shorts.

Alicia was just devouring Jackson's cock, or as much of it as she could get into her mouth. She was slobbering all over him and carrying on. She had one hand between her own legs, working her own pussy, which made her blowjob mission tougher.

Without giving it a second thought, I reached down and started rubbing Brad's dick through his shorts. He whipped his head around in shock, but offered no resistance.

"Brad, look at her," I whispered. "There's no way to stop her from fucking him now."

Alicia had given up on touching herself in favor of bucking her hips all over the place while sucking on Jackson. "God, I missed this cock!" she said, as she stroked it with both hands, getting it nice and hard for what she needed.

It did look awesome. I forgot my jealousy as I started lusting over Jackson's dick myself. Now that it was hard, it was jutting out *so* strong and thick. It really looked formidable.

As I worked my hand into Brad's zipper, Jackson had the good sense not to tell Alicia he had missed her pussy. But he clearly wanted her. I know that, because he was paying very little attention to me.

"He's going to fuck her, Brad … he's going to fuck her *so* well," I cooed as I stroked.

Alicia was stroking Jackson's cock furiously, as if daring him to cum. But it takes a lot of work to make Jackson cum— something that made him annoyingly proud.

As I casually stroked Brad, eager to see what Jackson and Alicia would do next, I sensed an escalation of breathing and spasms from Brad. Then I felt some unmistakable wet stuff on my hands.

"Oh Brad, you came already?" I said out loud without thinking.

Alicia and Jackson looked over and spontaneously laughed.

Perhaps it was a pathetic sight, Brad still fully clothed with cum all over his shorts.

"That's my Brad," Alicia said laughing, returning back to a vigorous jerk and suck on Jackson, as if to show Brad how much friction he could take.

Not wanting Brad to perish from embarrassment, I whispered in his ear, "Go take off your clothes, Brad. You don't want to miss this."

At my command, Brad obediently headed to the closet, which for some reason made my pussy twinge. I peeled my own clothes off until I was down to a bra and panties. The crotch of my white panties was already completely soaked. Self-conscious, I quickly pulled them off as well. Brad was back too, naked and awkward.

"Brad," I turned to him. "Help me with my bra,"

I turned my back to Brad as he fumbled with the clasp like a schoolboy. I giggled but then it was done.

Brad and I both stood behind the chair. Alicia was getting carried away with Jackson's blow job, working his balls with one hand while stroking with the other.

Even Jackson couldn't last too long with that kind of action. Alicia was playing with fire.

"No!" Jackson said, lifting Alicia up and tossing her on the bed. I didn't expect Alicia to like being tossed around like that, but she just squealed.

Jackson knelt over Alicia and spread her legs wide, leaning down to lick her pussy.

"Oh stop it, Jackson!" Alicia said. "I'm wet enough already. Brad can lick my pussy later. I want that dick!"

All of a sudden, the word popped out of me: "No!"

Alicia and Jackson paused, as if caught by their parents. They must have thought I was having a last-second crisis. But I was not.

"Brad, come here," I said, walking over to the bed.

Brad got up and walked dutifully toward us.

"Brad, I want you to put Jackson's cock inside her."

"Corrie," Alicia blurted out, "he's never done anything like that before."

I ignored her.

"Brad?" I gave him a stern look.

Alicia cocked her head, her expression curious, as if she wondered how far Brad could be pushed.

Probably a lot further than this, I thought as Brad dutifully grabbed Jackson's cock and put the tip of the head inside her.

I knew Jackson had let a couple of his male friends suck him off in school, so he was not intimidated by this kind of play.

"Thanks, Brad, I'll do the rest," said Jackson, nudging Brad aside.

Jackson pushed his cock inside Alicia. She was so turned on that he managed to push most of it in on the first stroke.

"Oh!" Alicia said, shocked into focus.

I sat down in the chair, propping my legs up on each side. I summoned Brad, who sat down between my legs, as if we were an old married couple. It honestly felt good to have him there.

Jackson was grinding with Alicia, working his dick around in circular motions. He was just toying with her at this point, getting her revved up.

Alicia, meanwhile, had her muscular legs wrapped firmly around him, pulling him deeper. It was amazing to see another woman taken by Jackson. I was fascinated by the similarities ... and the differences.

Alicia didn't put up as much resistance to Jackson's thrusts as I sometimes did. He was sliding most of his cock in and out of her rather easily. Her moans were happy, and she wasn't exactly feeling pain or being pushed to the limits. Not yet anyway.

In the bedside mirror, I could see Brad's hand moving. He was back to stroking himself, his face full of intensity and torment. I couldn't imagine what he was going through, watching the love of his life getting something so primal from a man who never took the groceries from her car or listened to her whine about her stepmother, much less put a ring on her finger. What she needed from my husband mocked his marriage with every thrust.

As Jackson picked up the pace, my interest level rose. How hard would he be able to pound her?

"Oh god, Jackson. Oh god!"

Pretty damn hard, evidently. Jackson had to be careful pounding me in missionary. I've never been able to take his whole dick in that position. Evidently Alicia didn't have that problem, *that little bitch*.

"Oh Jackson, you're hitting my deep spot!" Alicia cried out. I knew what she meant there. Now and then Jackson's penis would give me what I guess are called uterine orgasms.

He was really pounding her now, withdrawing halfway and then bucking in, pulling her off the bed. Then Alicia came, and it was like a seizure ripped through her body. She screamed and flailed on the mattress, her thighs shaking.

"Cummming!" she managed to blurt out in between spasms. It was only then I realized something I wished I'd noticed earlier: Jackson wasn't using condoms. That sucked. During one of our fights, he had insisted he always used condoms with Alicia.

Anyhow, I was too far gone to care, fingers circling my clit, legs splayed wide. Between my legs, I could see Brad's right arm jerking. I loved watching Jackson exert so much control over Alicia. Maybe Brad did too.

Alicia pulled Jackson all the way in, her legs urging him deeper even as her spasms subsided. I expected Jackson to pull out, perhaps switch positions. I usually needed a breather after a deep cervical orgasm like that, to let the warmth spread throughout my body. But Jackson kept thrusting, albeit at a less intense pace.

He leaned into her, and for an insecure minute I thought he would try to kiss her. But then Jackson put his head up: "Brad … towel … quick!" he called out.

Brad jumped up, his little dick poking in front of him as he raced into the master bath and came back with a beach towel. Jackson raised Alicia off the bed and Brad dutifully placed the towel under his wife, as if this was standard duty for husbands. Brad's submission to Jackson's commands made me tingle—fuck it, made me tingle times ten—and I knew my own orgasm was on its way.

Jackson and I had messy sex more often than not, but a towel seemed a bit extravagant. *I wouldn't put it past Alicia to be a control freak about her sheets*, I thought snarkily.

Brad sat back down between my legs and started working his cock again, as if he knew what was about to happen.

Jackson was fucking Alicia at a pretty decent pace again, but he wasn't trying to pound her into the bed. He seemed to be concentrating hard on his exact movement. Then, it happened.

"You're gonna squirt, Alicia. You're gonna squirt!"

Out of nowhere, Alicia seemed to expel Jackson's cock as he quickly pulled it out, jamming a couple fingers inside her and massaging her clit.

"Oh fuck!!" Alicia said before she unleashed so much fluid on Jackson it seemed like her pussy had a water gun in it. Surge after surge poured out of her, soaking the towel and Jackson's crotch as well.

Now I knew what that towel was for. In front of me I could see Brad's arms moving in a blur. He was jacking off his dick like a madman. Then he spasmed over the sound of Alicia's ecstatic coos.

I'd heard about girls squirting on big dicks before. I found myself resenting Alicia a little bit, though I wasn't envious of the mess. *That must feel so damn good*, I thought to myself. A few times I had leaked on Jackson's cock when I came—enough to make me think there might be a faucet in there somewhere. But I had never found a way to open it.

Once, while comparing notes about rare guys who know how to fuck, my friend Andrea told me about a couple of guys who knew how to make her squirt. She told me, "Corrie, it was like going to fucking heaven."

Heaven sounded pretty damn good, but Jackson had taken me close enough many times. So what made squirting different? I had pressed Andrea for more. "Gosh," she said, her face flushed. "Billy was fucking me pretty good; I had already cum hard a couple of times. His big dick was filling me *so* good." She paused. "Then I got the sense of being a bit bloated and uncomfortable, as if I need to purge something. I begged Billy to keep going, just like that, and Corrie, it was like a dam breaking. I pushed Billy's dick right out of my pussy along with all this juice!" Her smile was ecstatic. "All the stupid, stupid shit, all the stress in my life … it just flooded out of me. I stained my sister's bedspread and I knew she'd be pissed, but damn, Corrie, just imagine if you were holding something inside, and you became aware it was actually a *really big* something, and the fucking was pulling it out, and then every second of letting loose was like this huge release. Not just fluid, not just stress, but the *sweetest* pleasure." With a huge sigh, she added, "Squirting is so fucking good."

"Even if you ruin your sister's bedspread?" I asked, still grossed out by the idea of so much wetness. It sounded embarrassing.

"Oh, god yes, she was pissed!" Andrea giggled, clearly not sorry.

For months after that, I chased the squirting orgasm with Jackson. But I was finally forced to give up. I was over-thinking it. A couple times I thought I was aware of something deep that wanted to blow up. But it was not to be … and the sex was plenty good enough.

I jolted from Andrea back to reality as Alicia pushed Jackson back on the bed, attempting to mount him.

No!

"What do you think you're doing, bitch?" I told her, moving her aside. "It's my turn!"

Alicia couldn't really protest, could she? I started riding Jackson for all I was worth. Even though I couldn't take him as well as Alicia in this position, controlling the thrusts and bouncing on him, we could fuck with intensity. I loved it because all I had to do was fuck him as hard as I possibly could, taking care not to lift beyond the tip of this cock.

I felt so damn full this way. No need to worry about rubbing my clit. All we had to do was keep the rhythm going until I lost my shit. I was fucking Jackson really hard now, looking into his eyes. I loved his fierceness in that moment as he focused solely on working my body and pleasing me.

In their bedroom mirror, I could see Alicia standing behind us, next to Brad.

Alicia was whispering in Brad's ear while feverishly stroking him. I went back to fucking Jackson—I was so close now. My pussy made happy loud sucking noises as I raised up high and slammed myself down.

"I'm gonna fucking cum!" I told Jackson. I looked around at Brad and smiled … I have no idea why. He must have liked the view, or my smile, or something Alicia was saying in a teasing voice in his ear, because Brad came again, and I felt it wash over me. Not a squirt, but definitely what Jackson and I called a ten-bagger. Yes, that's even bigger than a mega-cum.

Ten-bagger was a term we learned while studying investing from Peter Lynch. That's a stock that exceeds its value by ten times. For Jackson and me, a ten-bagger took on a different meaning in the bedroom. It was the highest level of pleasure I could reach. A ten-bagger meant a full-body cum, guaranteed legs shaking and muscle spasms. And if I wasn't careful, I could strain my neck as my shoulders shook. Jackson tried to remember to hold me in place.

Well, I guess Brad liked the view of the ten-bagger, for he came hard. Having an audience must have upped the ante for me also. In my life so far, I'd only had a handful of those ten-baggers.

"You did it!" Jackson said supportively. He loved it when he felt my legs shake uncontrollably around his dick, probably because he knew I wouldn't make him do any work around the house for days after he fucked me like that.

I feel bad for any woman who hasn't experienced that lingering loose-body bliss.

I fondled my boobs for a moment—my nipples were always a bit tender after a cum like that. I could see a satisfyingly jealous look on Alicia's face. Her boobs were definitely smaller than mine, something I hadn't realized until we got naked. Then I collapsed on Jackson's chest, asserting my territory like a lioness on Animal Planet.

Jackson's penis was still hard inside me. Uncomfortably hard, to be honest. I slowly lifted myself off of it, laughing at the loud, gross-sounding plop as it exhaled the air from inside me. Those were supposed to be our private noises.

"Oh Jackson, that big dick needs to cum!" I said.

I kneeled on one side of Jackson, working his cock with both hands. His dick had such a nasty, sticky feeling. "Jackson, you are absolutely coated with pussy cum!" I said as I stroked. God that was fucking hot.

Before I could say anything, Alicia kneeled across from me. "There's enough for two here!" she insisted, pushing my left hand aside as she grabbed the base of Jackson's cock.

I'm not sure what came over me—maybe it was the excellence of my orgasm—but I was feeling generous. I let Alicia help out.

If you haven't jacked off a cock with another girl before, it actually takes practice to coordinate the stroking. But we started slow and got into it quickly.

Out of the corner of my eye, I saw Brad leaving the room. He shut the door a bit harder than he needed to.

Without stopping my stroke, I looked at Alicia quizzically.

"It's okay," she said. "He gets like that sometimes."

"Like what?" I asked, genuinely curious.

"I guess a bit jealous, or intimidated." The thought made my pussy clench a little bit.

"Thank you, Jackson," I said to him. "Thank you for fucking us so well."

Alicia joined in as we stroked. "Oh god, yes," she said. "You are a blessing."

"God, Jackson, you are such a fucking stud!" I said as Alicia and I worked to pick up the pace without losing our grips. "It takes both of us to handle your beautiful dick!"

"Oh fuck, yes!" Alicia said. We were moving as a blur now, with Jackson moaning underneath. "God, I love the way you make me squirt. My tiny-dicked husband has *never* made me squirt!"

I started laughing and—shocker—Jackson starting bucking and spasming, almost bumping me off the bed. I hadn't seen him cum so quickly in a long time, and I wasn't ready. The spurts shot up. One hit my face, one my chest. I pushed his cock toward Alicia, and the last few spurts found her belly. He soaked her but she didn't care.

"Oh Jackson I *love* watching you cum!" Alicia said. "You cum so much more than my husband!" Her fawning was starting to irritate me.

For some reason, I flashed to Daniel. I could capture all his cum in my hand. The first time I tried to do that with Jackson, I got it all over my red dress. Jackson's taboo biological superiority turned me on so much that I sucked him until he was hard again, ripped off that nasty red dress, and made him fuck me without a condom, yelling for him to "cum in me with your huge baby-maker!" *God, it turns me on to type this.* And yeah, I was pregnant with Chelsea soon after. So at least in his case, there was something to it.

Daniel had a lot more chances to make me pregnant before that. Whether Jackson reaching places Daniel couldn't hope to reach and soaking me with cum that I could literally feel on my back walls had anything to do with it, I'll leave that to the doctors. But it sure makes me wet to think that Jackson could do what another man couldn't.

Anyhow, Jackson got up to hit the shower and clean himself up. *It's a shame*, I thought as I found myself turned on again. Before I could say yes, no, or anything, Alicia was astride me, kissing and rubbing my breasts.

Chapter 9

Now, normally I'm not that into girls, but some girls can eat pussy like you wouldn't believe. The last girl between my legs was Andrea, years before she took her long blonde curls and relationship dramas to San Francisco. She would conquer a girl as soon as a guy, and once I gave in to her advances, I didn't regret it.

And here was Alicia, working her way in between my legs with an expertise that told me she'd done this before. No one had more incentive to please me than her, right? Talk about making amends! Snaking her tongue around my clit certainly counted.

Jackson came out the bathroom, towel around his waist, just in time to see my legs clamped around Alicia's head as I came in her face. Maybe I pulled her head into my pussy a little hard, I don't know, but Alicia seemed happy to submit. When I let her up, her face was slick with my juices and she wore a big, happy smile.

"Why, thank you, Alicia!" I said awkwardly, as if she had just dropped off a nice poinsettia. The three of us laughed, also awkwardly.

It's funny how the bliss of orgasm can quickly give way to mixed feelings. I was never very good at leaving Alicia's house, and this time was no exception. We didn't share many words as I got Jackson out the door with my own jeans quickly donned and zipped.

I didn't see Brad on the way out, and he didn't show his face. Fifteen minutes later, Jackson and I were sipping drinks at Starbucks.

"What just happened?" I asked him as he stirred his chai. And finally, we had a laugh without repercussions.

FOR A COUPLE OF weeks I didn't give Brad and Alicia much thought. But before too long, they started popping back into my mind. I was like that guy in the movie *Pi* trying to solve a crazy math formula. There was a riddle I hadn't figured out yet either. Back to the scene of the debauchery then ....

I insisted we do it again. This time, no one resisted. At least not to my face. Maybe Brad was unhappy about it, I don't know. I didn't care if I was putting Brad through the ringer—hell, he got some nice orgasms for his trouble! Three weeks later, same routine. Drinks on Alicia's patio—a bit less awkward this time. Then, a bit more pot—hand-rolled Jackson style—then, the bedroom.

But ... something was different. This time, as Jackson and Alicia began to get it on, Brad couldn't hide the conflicted look on his face. The last time we'd gotten together, he'd started out horny, excited. Now he seemed angry, upset. Alicia and Jackson didn't notice. They were already lost in their own erotic world, famished for each other.

Maybe Brad thought the last scene had been a one-time deal. Maybe it was beginning to dawn on him where this was all heading. Instead of sitting in the chair, he hightailed out of the room, slamming the door behind him.

The loud slam got the attention of Alicia, who took time away from caressing Jackson through his boxers to look up.

"I've got this, Alicia," I told her. "Don't worry."

Past the kitchen and down a short staircase, I found Brad in his "man cave." I couldn't miss it, thanks to the glow of the massive screens he had in there. There was Brad, already sunk into his recliner, flipping channels and looking petulant.

I grabbed the remote from his hand. "Brad, come over here." I said, patting the couch. Brad came dutifully over. I smiled to myself. I liked that Brad was obedient, perhaps in a way that he was not with Alicia. Even pissed off, he had no choice but to follow my directives. Or so it seemed to me. "Come on, it's okay," I added.

Brad's eyes welled up. Next thing I knew, he was crying on my shoulder, and I was consoling him. When I held him closer, the tears flowed faster.

Sobs erupted as I cooed into his ear. But Brad didn't need someone to feel bad for him. Fine by me, because I was *not* feeling bad for Brad.

"It's okay, Brad, it's okay," I whispered as he cried.

The sobs abated.

"What's wrong, honey?" I asked. I suddenly realized I felt closer to Brad than to men I'd known far longer. Brad had exposed himself in just about every way, stripped away his manhood in front of me. That takes guts.

"I'm going to lose her," Brad exhaled. A few more sobs. I wiped his snotty face with a Kleenex. Suddenly, Brad looked boyishly cute to me, in a guy-from-tech-support kind of way.

"Can't you see? She's falling in love with Jackson," he spit out.

I'm not gonna lie—it was a verbal slap. But even though Jackson drives me nuts sometimes, I knew deep down Brad was wrong. Across the house, we could hear Alicia starting to yell and moan, her cries attempting to contradict me.

"Well, first off, Brad, that's not going to happen."

"How do you know?"

"First off, I'm not going to let them fuck again. *Maybe* one more time, if they're lucky."

"But … they'll just find a way. Jackson said—"

"Yes, well I don't care what Jackson says," I replied. "I know I can't control Jackson's cock like Alicia does yours …."

Brad blushed.

"But I can certainly stop him from fucking a particular person. Jackson loves me, Brad. I've never doubted that. Yes, he is stubborn about fucking other women," I conceded. "It's getting harder to deny him that." I shook my head. "Even harder after watching what he does for them." He flinched, telling me I had hit a sore spot.

We actually had to stop for a minute to let Alicia's screams subside. She was clearly orgasming now. *Probably squirting, that fucking horny bitch.* More twitching from Brad's cock, which was poking against his zipper.

"Brad, pretty soon Jackson will be history for you and Alicia. He'll still be giving me some problems, but those will be *my* problems."

"You think so?" Brad asked hopefully.

"But Jackson's leaving doesn't begin to solve your problem, Brad," I went on.

Brad gave me a quizzical look. And then it hit me: I knew exactly what I needed to do.

"Let me show you what I'm talking about."

I got up, shut the man cave door to keep Alicia's screams at bay, and knelt in front of Brad. I started working on his zipper.

"Wha-wha-what are you doing?" Brad protested—kind of.

"Exactly what you wanted, Brad, what you need."

With that, I had his cock out of his fly and firmly in hand.

"Oh my god!" Brad called out.

He hardened immediately.

"This is your problem, Brad," I said, jerking him with my thumb and index finger. "This is the source of your problem with Alicia—your little penis!"

It really was tiny. It couldn't have been much more than four inches, and it was as hard as it was ever going to get.

Without warning, Brad spurted helplessly in my hand and onto my shirt.

"Oh Jeezus, Brad!" I scolded him. "I liked this shirt!"

Brad looked sheepish.

I didn't let him off the hook, either. "Wow, Brad, what a tiny, ineffective penis you have."

Brad's face flashed a look of shame. And worry. But I wasn't going anywhere. I stood up as if to give him a lap dance, shimmying my shirt off, slow and sexy, letting Brad get his first private look at my breasts. His eyes widened. I tossed the cum-stained shirt aside.

"See, Brad, this is the problem," I said. "Now that Alicia has been fucked by a *man* like Jackson, your marriage is never safe." I paused. "C'mon, Brad, you know *exactly* what I'm talking about."

Brad gave me a fearful look.

"You know what I'm talking about Brad, don't you? Don't you?!"

A moment's hesitation, then, finally … a nod. "Sometimes I wish she wasn't … such a slut!" he blurted out.

"Oh, there's more to it than that, Brad," I said. I started working his penis again, coaxing it back toward erection, starting gently. He exhaled. "Fuck, your dick is tiny, Brad! Look how I'm stroking it with just a couple of fingers. It's so thin …. It takes two hands to make Jackson's cock cum. And you have to work at it." I clicked my tongue. "And … he cums so much more than your little boy penis does!"

I was teasing him, but not really. Biology can be cruel as hell. Brad thrust his hips as his erection firmed. He was over his sexual shock and heading toward another cum.

"Brad, let me demonstrate," I said. The thought of what I was about to do gave me a rush of naughty, cruel power.

I was already shirtless; taking off my skirt didn't take much, just an extra tug across my big hips, and then swiveling out. Brad looked like a kid at Disney World. Next, my panties, and soon I was leaning on the side of the couch, my ass raised high in the air.

"C'mon, Brad, take this pussy!"

I moved my ass around in a slow, teasing circle—a trademark move that would have had Jackson slamming into me in an instant. But Brad hesitated.

"Brad, c'mon! Your wife is getting her brains fucked out. She isn't thinking about you. Get over here and fuck me!"

Still hesitant, but plenty hard, Brad came up behind me. He had to tiptoe a bit to line his cock up.

"Put it in me Brad!"

I had to suppress a laugh as Brad fumbled like a virgin around my opening.

I wasn't sure if he was inside, but then I thought I felt something. I looked back; Brad had pushed up against me.

"Are you in, Brad?"

"I … yes," he said.

"Then give it to me, Brad! Take this pussy!"

Brad tried to fuck me, but from this standing angle, he couldn't keep it in. I thought I felt something for a second, but then he was out again.

God, I can be diabolical. I suddenly recalled how much Daniel had struggled to take me like this. In my catharsis, I almost called Brad "Daniel."

"Okay, that's not going to work," I said. I guided Brad to the couch and sat him down.

I put my thighs on Brad's lap so that his dick was leaning in front of me, though it was barely hard anymore. I reached down to solve that problem.

"What's wrong, Brad?"

"I … I guess I'm nervous."

"Well, Brad, you should be nervous. I'm a hot girl who needs to be fucked, and I expect you to do it properly."

My fingers seemed to have an electric effect on his dick—he was getting hard in record time.

"Brad, have you ever seen Jackson fuck Alicia from behind like we did?"

"Yes …" he said.

"Was she screaming and yelling?"

"Oh god, yes," Brad said.

"Did he have any trouble falling out?"

"No …" Brad admitted.

"You see, Brad," I said as I stroked him, "girls need to have their pussies used and taken. They need to be pounded, filled, to scream and cum. And your thin little dick can't do that. You know that, right Brad? Deep down, you know that."

"Yes …" he moaned. It gave me so much satisfaction to hear Brad confess this that I felt my own pussy dripping.

"Brad, did you notice how often you slipped out of me?"

"Yes …."

"That's not how you make a pussy cum. And the thing is, doggy isn't even a difficult position for a *real* man. There are so many positions guys like you can't even use, because your little dicks can't reach. Guys like Jackson have a huge fucking advantage over you. And once they learn how to use that advantage," I added, twisting the knife, "then they go after hot women like your wife."

Brad moaned.

"Even if she promises to be faithful to you, she can't," I said. "Trust me on this one, Brad." I slowly stroked him and then let go, careful not to get him too excited. I wasn't done with him yet.

I got off the couch, keeping my pose seductive, enjoying Brad's depraved look as he filmed my naked breasts with his eyes, as if he knew he might not get another chance.

"You like what you see, Brad?" I said, looking him right in the eye as I bent over him and swayed.

He looked away, kind of ashamed, but he didn't stop stroking either.

"Do you like this pussy, Brad?" I asked him, rubbing my

fingers down between my thighs to give him a closer look as I pried my lips open for him.

"Oh, yeah!" Brad said.

I loved watching him stroke his little dick. Lots of Brads must have done that over the years, imagining my naked body. But this was the first time I had actually seen it with my own eyes.

"This pussy needs a good fucking, Brad," I said. I rubbed my fingers down, feeling the electric pull from my cunt. "Do you think you can please this tight little pussy, Brad?" I kept my eyes locked with his.

His hesitation said it all. "Let's see what you can do, Brad…." With that, I quickly straddled him, towering over his white-collar body. "Let's see how well you fuck."

Without waiting for Brad to answer, I guided his little dick inside. It took concentration and finger holding to get him in—very different from Jackson. where I could just give his big head a nudge.

But then Brad was inside me.

I started rocking up and down, careful not to raise my hips too far. I could only go up a couple inches with each thrust or he'd fall out.

I put my hands on his shoulders. I felt less like I was riding him, and more like I was pushing him into the couch.

Brad moaned.

"See, Brad? You're fucking me!"

"Oh god!" Brad called out.

"Brad, does my pussy feel good?"

"Oh yes!"

"I can't feel your little dick at all. Nothing, Brad!"

That wasn't completely true; I could feel a very mild tickle and sometimes a small pleasure when I pressed down on him, but it was true enough to twist the knife in Brad.

I said, "This isn't fucking, Brad!" I wiggled easily up and down on his dick. "With Jackson, by now I'd be slamming up and down on his pole, fucking him till my legs shook. But if I slam on you," I raised my legs up a bit to prove the point, "your tiny dick slips out."

And it was true. His dick wasn't in me anymore.

Brad's expression reflected a weird mix of desire and utter despair.

I was using him, crushing him, but I couldn't stop myself.

I worked his cock up and down outside my pussy with my fingers, trying to keep him hard and not intimidate him into a noodle.

"You see, Brad, you can't please a woman like this. Not when she needs a real fucking!"

Brad moaned.

"Jackson makes me bounce on him until it hurts, until I beg him to let me make him cum."

Brad's face flashed shame and desire. "I can last ..." he said, defiantly.

"What?" I asked him, surprised he dared say anything.

"I can last ... until you feel good."

"Oh Brad. I'm sorry, but there's no way."

"Here ... I'll show you," Brad pleaded.

"Brad, there's no chance you can last more than a couple minutes inside my pussy."

"Oh yes I can!" Brad insisted, as if holding onto the last shred of the alpha male he once was—or thought he was. Please let me try to please you."

It was important to Brad, so I let him try. But I knew that the way I was grinding and the high degree of self-control I had, he was bound to fail.

"Brad, your tiny dick is going to squirt so fast inside."

He groaned but then grabbed my shoulders, trying like hell to hold me down on him further. I made a point of keeping the thrusts close, knowing that if I somehow kept him inside me, he wouldn't last.

I started laughing. "Brad, you're tickling me! Cum for me, Brad. Squirt your little boy penis!"

"Oh …" he moaned.

"Doesn't matter, Brad, don't try to last. Your little dick could fuck me for an hour and I still wouldn't cum." I stared right into his eyes so he'd know I wasn't just saying that to make him excited. I meant every fucking word.

"That's it … squirt!" I sat down on him hard.

Brad's face lost its determination, and looking helpless, he squirted, just as I'd predicted.

"Brad, that's it? When Jackson cums, he blasts all over the back of my walls …. I couldn't even feel your little spurts."

I sat down on him, but not before removing his ineffective penis. No, Brad wasn't wearing a condom. But I was confident he hadn't impregnated me with his small, ineffective load. I wiped it on Brad's T-shirt. *I know, classy.*

Then I sat down next to him, still giggling at his pathetic attempt at fucking.

Before I could say anything else mean to him, Brad started to cry again.

In an instant, my mood shifted. I pulled him onto my shoulder again, comforting him.

"It's not fair," Brad said. "I love her so much."

"And you want to be everything she needs," I said, completing his thought, if not his sentence.

"Yesssss …." Brad was almost sobbing now.

"Brad, I know this is hard, but honestly, you are lucky. Alicia just adores you."

"But I … I never wanted this," he insisted.

"And I never wanted Jackson to fuck other girls like your wife!" I said to him, sitting him up straight. "Brad, you have to be strong. Just like I need to be."

I handed him a Kleenex from the lamp table.

"Just like you want to be all things to Alicia, I want Jackson to be all things to me. But he's not."

"He … isn't?"

"Well, for one thing, he can't—no, refuses—to keep his dick in his pants."

We both laughed at the obviousness of that, though Alicia's moans had finally subsided.

"But that's not all, Brad." Brad looked at me attentively, as if his own marriage hung on my every word.

"Jackson, well, he lacks a certain sensitivity. He's a good man, but ... before him, I was in love with a guy who was, well, a lot like you, Brad. He was so thoughtful and sweet, and we had this deep emotional connection. Nobody took care of me like my Daniel."

I hadn't mentioned Daniel's name to anyone else in a long time.

I realized I was selling Daniel short. "But that's not all, Brad. Daniel was really fucking smart, and really successful. He deserved way more than I gave him."

"But ... you broke up with him?"

"Yes, I did," I admitted. "I left him for Jackson. But ... sometimes regret it." I had never confessed this before, or even thought through it. But as the words left my mouth, I could hear their truth. "And even when I don't regret it, I miss him. I miss the feeling of being best friends, of sharing ... almost everything." I was silent for a moment, remembering. "Even stupid things," I continued, "like when we took long road trips, Daniel would lie down and put his head in my lap. Jackson ... he would never do anything like that. It was just a closeness Daniel and I had."

Brad was fascinated.

"Maybe ..." I said, "maybe one reason I am so mad at you and Alicia is because, well, the more I spend time with the two of you, the more I realize I could have done it differently. Instead of leaving Daniel, maybe I could have committed to him and had someone on the side if I got super horny, kind of like you and Alicia. It just ... well, the kind of relationship you and Alicia have never occurred to me. I never imagined the other possibilities. Maybe," I confided to Brad, "I chose the wrong husband."

"But Corrie," Brad protested. "I've seen you and Jackson together, and I've heard Jackson talk about you. You have more than a sexual thing. You have a child, and you have, at least as far as I can tell, some kind of bond."

"Yes," I acknowledged. "The bond has grown. It started with the sex, but something else has built up. And he does have this way of making me feel like a woman, like I belong on his arm … but I'm at a crossroads, Brad. Because I always dreamed of a monogamous partner, you know—the Prince Charming who pulls you onto his horse—Richard Gere carrying you out of the factory. In those fantasies, there are *never* two men riding away with the same girl." We both smirked at the absurdity of the image.

I continued, "I don't think I realized what it would do to me, to have to sacrifice that Prince Charming ideal, that one guy who is my everything. It really makes me crazy."

"Crazy horny?" asked Brad.

"Yeah, I guess, crazy horny, but also just plain crazy, as you have seen."

"And so we're here …" Brad said.

"And so we're here," I agreed. We smiled at each other, laughed and hugged a bit. It was strange to be hugging him after how cruel I had been. But it felt completely right.

"I hope you figure it out," Brad said. "I think you will. I think you and Jackson … have a future together. I'm not sure how, but I just think you guys work as a couple."

"Thanks, Brad." I needed to hear someone else say that, given all our turmoil.

"You've been so … honest with me. Like no other woman has—not even Alicia."

"I hope I didn't upset you, Brad," I said.

"Well, you did. I can't deny that."

"Brad, I just wanted you to really understand what Alicia needs, so that you can be more at peace with your … arrangement."

"Well, I guess you did that," Brad said. We both laughed again. I suddenly felt shy. But I pushed the shyness back; I knew what he needed to hear. "And Brad, I just wanted you to understand. It isn't like Alicia is some kind of obsessed size queen. What she wants is what … most women want. Even if we're really bad at admitting it, even to ourselves. Do you understand that, Brad? It's really important that you do."

"I … I think so." Brad said.

I grabbed some more Kleenexes, wiping more of his cum off him. In doing so, I brushed up against his penis again and realized it was almost hard again already.

Brad and I weren't quite done after all.

Chapter 10

I STARTED STROKING BRAD's penis to full hardness.

"Look Brad," I said, going right back into teasing mode. "I only need two fingers to stroke that little tiny dick." It felt perfectly natural for me to talk like this to him. It didn't even feel mean anymore. We were almost like a couple of girlfriends who had exposed it all to each other.

"Brad, let's review this one more time," I said forcefully as I stroked him a bit faster.

"Why is Alicia fucking Jackson in the other room?"

"Because she's a slut!" Brad exhaled.

"Uh, no, Brad. That's not why. Tell me why, Brad. You know why."

He looked at my breasts longingly, then back down. He moaned.

"It's okay, Brad, you can touch them," I teased. "As long as you answer me."

Like a clumsy adolescent, Brad greedily grabbed at my right tit. It made me smile, but I was also flattered. I suddenly realized I could help Brad in his marriage, but I'd have to take it further.

"Answer me, Brad!"

"Because I'm … small," he said.

"That's right, Brad."

"Tell me more, Brad! Tell me why she needs it so bad that she fucked her good friend's husband!"

"Because I'm too small."

"Too small for Alicia."

"Yes."

"But that's not all, Brad." I stopped stroking him.

He moaned in disappointment.

"You want to cum, Brad?"

"Oh, so bad!" he said.

"You want to me to make you cum?"

"Oh god, yes!"

"Then tell me why Alicia needs to fuck Jackson."

"Because I'm too small!"

"Yes," I said, "but there's more."

"Because she needs to cum hard!"

"Yes," I said. "Good. But there's still more. I'm not making you cum until you say it, Brad." I had my hand away from his dick, rubbing his thigh to keep him on edge.

"Because …."

He paused. Then he got it. Small as he was, Brad was sharp as hell.

"Because I'm too small to fuck pussies?"

"Yes!" I said. "Not just Alicia's pussy. But most pussies. Maybe all pussies. So there's no point in being mad at Alicia just because you are inadequate, is there?"

"No."

"And she needs fucking very badly, doesn't she?"

"Oh yes."

"Without someone like Jackson … without your arrangement … she would cheat on you. You understand that, right?"

"Yes …."

"It's not that she doesn't love you. She just … needs it. Needs it so bad!"

I reached for Brad's tiny penis again and put a few fingers around it, marveling at how I could encompass him so easily.

He moaned as I started stroking him.

"Say it again, Brad," I commanded.

"I'm too small," Brad said.

"Too small for what?"

"Too small for … pussies!"

"Say it again, Brad!"

"I'm too small for pussies!"

Totally in control of Brad now, I pulled my hands away. His look was desperate.

"Please, don't stop," Brad said. I smiled at the way he thrust his hips up, searching out my fingers.

"Only if you say it louder, Brad," I said to him in my sternest voice.

"I'm too small for pussies!" Brad called out, loudly.

"That's better!" I said, grabbing his dick between three fingers and pulling hard. I marveled as his small size. As hard as it was, his dick was even smaller than Daniel's.

I started stroking faster, thrilled to have so much power over his cock, over all of him.

He moaned helplessly.

"Brad, do you want to cum?"

"Oh god, more than anything!"

"Then I want you to yell it … loud enough for Alicia to hear."

I kept stroking him, egging him on with my touch.

"Okay," he said helplessly. Finally he called out, "I'm too small for pussies!"

"Louder, Brad!"

"I'm too small for pussies!!"

"Fucking louder, Brad!!"

"I'm too small for pussies!!!"

This time he really screamed it.

"Okay, Brad, squirt that tiny dick!"

I was shaking his cock in a blur, totally blanketing his tiny dick in my fist. He was not going to hold out much longer.

"Oooohh!!"

And out came the squirts, urgent and fast, peppered by his cries.

"That's it, Brad," I cooed, continuing to stroke his penis, reveling in my ability to make him cum at will. "Did that feel good, Brad?"

"Oh my god … yes."

"I'm glad. Not much cum in that tiny dick," I teased. "You've seen Jackson cum, right?"

"Yes …" he said sheepishly

"And?"

I was still casually stroking, surprised to feel him twitching already.

"You felt like a little boy, didn't you Brad?" I asked, still stroking.

"Yes …" Brad said. I could see a pleading look in his eyes, as if he wanted me to make him cum again, and again, and again.

"Brad, I think that's enough for today," I said, cleaning some cum off my hands and handing him the Kleenex box. "You can always get back to this later." I started putting my clothes back on. "Let's go see what Jackson and Alicia are up to, shall we?"

Brad nodded, and rose to get dressed as well. It did not feel awkward in the least, like sex usually does with someone new. I felt compelled to give Brad one more hug.

"Thanks, Brad. That was … really good for me."

"Uh, me too," Brad said. I loved how he was okay being so completely naked with me. Maybe he and I could be friends.

With that, I grabbed his hand and opened the door, guiding him through the hallway.

Jackson and Alicia were dressed and scrubbed, sitting at the kitchen table and drinking Earl Grey as if they were book club members. They must have heard Brad yelling, but if they did, they didn't let on—a compassionate gesture on their part. Brad's face was red enough as it was.

I'm not going to lie and claim this moment wasn't weird. With the four of us, it almost always was. Too many crossed wires. I refused Alicia's offer of tea, and within a few minutes, Jackson and I were driving home again, leaving Alicia and Brad's relationship more complicated than where we found it.

Chapter 11

THAT WAS ABOUT IT for the drama of Jackson and Alicia. To my knowledge, they never fooled around again. Brad and I, however, continued along the path toward friendship. I think it bothered Jackson a little, but he couldn't say dick about it.

It was odd having coffee with Brad at the Java Roaster, or lunch on the sub shop patio when things got warmer. Brad was a genuinely decent guy. I think he reveled in our lack of secrets. If only my marital problems could be solved so easily.

After Alicia/Brad, Jackson and I weren't back yet. Touch and go was the new normal. Jackson alternated between trying to win back my trust and expressing his mounting frustration. His "I always get the girl in the end" patience was tested. I knew I had uncovered some clues to my marital mystery. Other puzzle pieces eluded me.

One night when Jackson and I were up too late, camped out at our kitchen table, he swore up and down he would not cheat again. There was no way I could really believe that. Not now. I'm not sure he believed it either. The only times we found closeness was when our daughter was around. Cheering her on at band events or dance recitals seemed like the only thread connecting us.

It was strange to feel so dry between my legs—even when Jackson walked around in his briefs. Watching him do household chores while his muscles casually rippled had once been a surefire way to warm me up. Now, watching Jackson putting away silverware was just ... Jackson putting away the silverware.

I'm still not certain how Jackson went without sex while we were so distant; maybe he jerked off a lot. I'm pretty sure he didn't cheat. Would that last? Especially when I was keeping him at bay, and rather coldly at that. The memories of our encounters with Alicia and Brad lingered. When sleep eluded me, I found myself masturbating to the scenes in my head, rotating fingers until I lost it. As sleep drifted in, I'd wonder how I'd become such a dysfunctional mess.

I needed something to pull me out of marital purgatory. A few months later, that something came in the form of my college friend Lisa. Lisa had married at an early age—twenty-two—then divorced. I'd never liked her ex, Walter. For one thing, I didn't like how Walt looked at me when we were out together. Some guys stare in a harmless, flirty way. He stared in a greedy way, like he would cheat on Lisa in a second, which he did, just not with me.

They divorced, childless, when Lisa was twenty-five. Now twenty-seven, she'd moved closer to my area in search of work, and maybe a new life. I was glad to have a new girl pal, especially with Jackson and me on the outs.

But her "guess who's back?" text message still threw me. I was a bit afraid of the trouble Lisa could get me into. Back when I knew her, wild times were the rule.

Lisa and I made plans to drink and catch up Friday—the same evening as Jackson guy's night out. They had taken to driving to the casino across state lines once a month. Jackson would roll in when the morning light was peeping in, sleep-deprived, too played out to do anything but crash. These days, that was fine by me.

I'd take a big whiff of Jackson's casino binges once the snores kicked in. He always smelled of cigarettes and beer overflow … but never of perfume. Somehow he was holding out. Jackson's fidelity was the only expression of love I accepted then; he was smart enough to know it.

Out with Lisa, I worried about alcohol. I don't drink much anymore. Lisa was always disappointed when you didn't take the shot glasses she pushed in your direction. But it wasn't as easy for me to stay in shape. Alcohol always led me down a binging/smoking path that left me sluggish and in no mood to exercise.

When I cut out the drinking, the lifestyle changed with it. My attempts to stay closer to my ideal weight were successful. Yeah, my hips were a bit wider, but Jackson liked it that way. Plus, being a mom had sunk in. Somehow I had to keep Lisa— or was it me?—in check.

I slithered into a red cocktail dress I'd bought recently. It was the kind of dress married women probably shouldn't wear when their husbands aren't around, but I liked the way it felt on my body.

I've always been a bit self-conscious about my ass; it required extra shopping to find jeans that didn't make me feel like an elephant from behind. This dress made me feel sleek— rounded, but not ridiculous. Guys objected to my curvy butt a lot less than I did, but it comes down to how you feel when you move across the room. This was a "move across the room" dress.

I wore a bra that pushed up my breasts, not that they needed much help. If anything, my breasts were getting a little bigger with age—though the drooping I could do without. Thank god for the push-up bra. I knew I'd be getting a few stares tonight, not that it would be easy to earn them around Lisa.

Lisa was one of those girls who was really skinny, with all the fat on her body impossibly landing on her tits. She wasn't tall—I would have said five-four, given I was a few inches taller. But she had striking dark hair and angular features that brought to mind an Egyptian goddess. The only concession I made for Lisa—no heels. She hated it when I wore heels. "You make me look like a damn midget!" she'd snarl.

Ah, and I had the perfect red heels for this outfit. I looked at them longingly, opting for black loafers instead. On the fun side, subtracting those four-inch heels would make me more approachable. When I go out in my highest heels, I'm close to six feet tall; only the tallest and cockiest men have the guts to approach me. *My feet will thank me on the other side*, I thought. I took one more look at my ass, talked myself up with a "fuck me if you think you can handle me" as I wiggled in the bedroom mirror, and headed out.

Lisa and I picked up where we left off. We plowed through dinner before settling into the corner table of a hopping techno bar. It was a good spot to talk/shout amongst ourselves, swatting away boys.

Lisa was her usual mixture of alluring and intimidating. I was surprised to see that she had worn a bulkier shirt than usual. I'd expected to see her tits on display. I was a bit disappointed that they were restrained, subdued, offering those around her no clue as to how gorgeous those breasts looked when they were bouncing free—now *that* was a sight to behold—but her skirt was short, and her legs were hot. I had to stop myself from dwelling on a couple college nights when I had pushed those thighs apart myself ....

Relief! Lisa didn't force a shot on me that night. To be honest, I probably drank more gin and tonics than she did. Guys hit on us a little bit, but they were quickly turned off by our intense girly chatter. As the beat droned on, our conversation turned toward career, dispensed with that, and went to the jugular.

"So Lisa, have you been getting any?" I asked her.

"Corrie! That's none of your business, hoochie."

"Since when? It always used to be my business."

"I guess you're right about that," Lisa replied. I expected her to talk about some hot new boyfriend, but instead she paused and made a doleful face. "To tell you the truth, single life hasn't been that great. I don't want a relationship right now, but the flings I've had … well, they haven't exactly rocked my world."

"Good cock is hard to find," I joked, thinking of my own ups and downs.

"No lie," she said. "But it's not just that. I get attracted to certain guys, but it's a superficial thing. And before you know it, they're glomming onto me." I remembered this phenomenon from college—guys getting a kiss from Lisa and deciding she was their future wife. Then the obsessive phone calls began.

"There was this one guy …" Lisa said. "I thought I'd hit the jackpot. He was a professional snowboarder, of all things. Free-spirited dude, but sweet as hell. He wasn't your typical doormat guy you can boss around…" Lisa hesitated.

I leaned in to get the good stuff. "You're not stopping now," I scolded.

"Okay. Well, he was up in my business from the beginning, assertive. The first time we were alone together, he pushed me back without any messing around, and had my skirt up. Before we'd even kissed he was eating some of the best"—Lisa looked around to see who was listening—"*pussy* I've ever had. I was cumming so damn hard. He had this long blond hair and I was grabbing it and pulling him up to me and yelling, 'Eat it! Eat it!'"

I almost lost it and did a spit take.

"It was hot!" Lisa insisted. "Corrie, I'm telling you, his tongue was in *command*, and there was something so … well, he had technique but … it's like he was *starving* for me. He made me feel like I was yummy enough to be eaten whole. I was so damn wet. I felt like a river down there, spread my legs and begged him to take me, and he did, but …."

"But …."

"Well, his penis was just sooo small." I thought I saw our beefcake bartender's lips twitch.

"Maybe it's because I was so freaking wet, but I couldn't feel anything down there. It was so disappointing. Especially after three weeks of flirting and late-night phone calls and—"

"Sister, we've all been there," I said reassuringly.

"Yeah, well, I kept him around for quite a while, because he really knew how to go down," Lisa said, leaning toward me. "I mean, he would stand above me and move my legs wide, and it was like he was directing an orchestra or something, and I was the damn violin!"

I started faking the performance with broad bow gestures while we howled.

"But then I wanted to fuck! And he couldn't finish me." Silence. "I'm starting to think I shouldn't have sex," she said finally, shaking her head.

"Why?" I asked her. "Your body is made for it!"

"If only guys didn't have so much trouble finding their way around me!" she said. "Am I really that hard to please?" She struck a pose, showing her biceps.

I laughed, but I was thinking, *If I was a guy, I might be a little intimidated by her swagger*. I didn't tell Lisa that.

"Well, when I'm by myself, I can self-service okay."

"Lisa!" I said, feigning righteous indignation.

"But when I'm with a guy, say, like Tiny Surfer"—cackles from both of us—"let's just say, he can eat it real good. Yeah, that is awesome, but then, guys just … well, I don't really cum from intercourse anyway, so why should I even care if he's small? It feels good, but I end up, I don't know, restless. Like I'm over-thinking sex. Thinking something is wrong with me. Thinking … maybe sex is overrated."

"Overrated?" I asked, astonished.

"Yeah, a little bit!" Lisa said.

I gave her my best therapist look, even though I'm the furthest thing from a therapist.

"Maybe you just need someone who doesn't shoot as soon as he is granted entry," I joked. More laughter and another smirk from the bartender.

"I've been dating a guy on and off who can go for a pretty long time," Lisa said. "Sometimes I have to ask him to stop." She drifted into thought, then came back. "Sore but not satisfied," she finished.

"Sore but not satisfied!" we both called out together, way too loud. I almost peed from laughing as I gripped my chair.

You had to be there. Or maybe it was the gin and tonics.

In the middle of all this, I got a text from Jackson. I didn't want to stop this chat, but I checked to make sure all was well with our daughter, who was at her new best friend's place. Turns out Jackson wasn't at the casino after all. *No casino. Flat tire. Back home*, was all he wrote.

A few of the guys who still hadn't left looked over at us. I don't think they quite believed what they'd heard coming from our table. They gave us big drunken smiles to support our raunchiness, which they probably thought would blow back on them before the evening was done.

One of the guys—he had a confident graduate student look, perfect for a certain "muscular professor" fantasy I have—cast an extra glance our way,

"So this new guy—the one who can 'love you a long time'—what's his name?" I asked.

"Oh. Nick ..." Lisa said, then ... "*Nick* ..." and she heaved a sigh.

"What's the problem with Nick?"

"That's the problem," Lisa said with some resignation. "There really is no problem. He's cute, he's a practicing lawyer, and he's not a schmuck. He works for a legal defense fund for battered women. You know, he's one of *those* guys, guys you can respect."

"Husband material," I offered.

"Yes! Exactly the kind of guy you and I talked about in

college, one of the really decent ones who is so hard to come by. I'm not sure what my problem is. Maybe I'm just not ready for something serious, and that's why we're not clicking sexually. Or maybe I just need to tell him where my spots are."

Lisa and I exchanged a wicked smile. We had discussed our "spots" before.

"Do you think he wants to date more seriously?"

"Yeah." She sighed again. "He doesn't like it that I still see other people." Lisa drew herself up in that arrogant way I loved. She rarely gave up sexual control to a man. Thinking about her matter-of-factly laying out the terms of her relationship to Nick—take it or leave it—made me tingle. Lisa could get away with stuff like that.

"Except …." Lisa looked at me, seeming to debate whether to continue. She took another swig from her drink as I nudged her leg under the table, encouraging her to dish. "Well, sometimes he does ask me about other guys. He even asked me about their cocks once, how they fucked."

"What did you say?"

"I told him it didn't matter because they were all quick cummers. He could fuck the longest."

"In other words, you took the path of least male ego damage," I teased.

Lisa sighed again. "Yeah, I guess so. Damn it! I think I'm back to the vibrator."

As I watched the laughter rippling through Lisa's elegant body, I thought, *God what a waste, a woman like that giving her orgasms to a machine.*

Right on cue, Muscular Librarian headed our way, staring right at her.

"Oh god," Lisa said, "you have to get him away. I think I'm too drunk for anything like this tonight."

"Don't worry," I said to Lisa, "I know how to handle this guy."

"Can I buy you ladies a drink?" he said, holding his Budweiser out, as if to remind us he wasn't the kind of guy to get a pretentious mixed drink.

"Why, does it look like we need one?" I asked him flirtingly, pointing to the dozen or so glasses on the table between us.

"Ah, yes … maybe not," he conceded.

My moment had arrived. "Tell me something …" I looked up.

"James," he said.

"James," I said. "Did you come over here because you want to talk to us, or, because … you want to fuck?"

Lisa's eyes popped. James' bottle of Bud almost flew out of his hands. He looked a little flushed, but give James-the-Aspiring-Stud credit, he didn't skip many beats before looking boldly at Lisa.

"I want to fuck."

"James, bravo for honesty!" I said. Lisa and I both clapped. But she was staring at me, dumbfounded. Back in the day, she'd always been the bold one.

"James," I grabbed his hand, "now that we've established that you want to fuck, tell us … how big is your cock?"

Lisa gasped but quickly got herself under control, curious to hear his answer. James seemed taken aback. We looked up at him expectantly.

"That's a little too much information for you to handle," he said, trying to dodge my thrust.

"Oh, I don't think so," I said. "James, you said you want to fuck. How can we make an informed decision on whether or not to fuck you, if we don't know what you're working with?"

I was smiling, but James seemed to sense I was serious.

"Well, let's just say I've never had any complaints," he said.

"Ah, but have you had any compliments?" I asked.

"I can handle my business!" James said, indignant.

"Oh, I see you can," I retorted. I had to defuse the situation before it got too ridiculous. "James, here's the deal, I went on. "I'm married, but my friend here, well, she's not, and I'm currently reviewing applications for a guy to fuck the living hell out of her. If you don't mind waiting with your friends, we'll get back to you."

Lisa smiled at him reassuringly, kicking me under the table.

James smiled a steely smile before heading down the bar to rejoin his posse.

Feeling a little bad, I waved and smiled so that his friends would think he'd made a lasting impression.

"Corrie!" Lisa admonished, once he was out of earshot.

"Well, you said you wanted me to get rid of him … so I did!"

"Yeah but … he was really cute." Lisa sighed, no doubt thinking of her vibrator.

"Oh, don't worry about him," I told her. "I did you a favor."

"And how's that?" Lisa asked, suspiciously.

"A guy who is truly mind-blowing in bed would have answered those questions differently," I assured her.

"And how's that?"

My mind raced back to the first time I'd met Jackson. And suddenly, I had an idea. A very nasty, exciting idea.

"Lisa, now's our chance … let's make a run for it!"

James was about thirty feet away, his back turned. His pals were laughing it up, still glancing in our direction. Lisa caught her purse strap on the chair, but she managed to pull it free without a ruckus, and soon we were scrambling out the back, laughing and huffing and running the few blocks till we got to our cars.

"Sorry we didn't get you laid," I told her.

"Oh, you're not sorry at all! The mouth on you …. I've *never* heard you talk like that."

"Sorry, sweetie, I'll make it up to you. Promise!"

"You'd better!" Lisa said.

Lisa insisted we call a cab and leave the cars for tomorrow. I went along with it—no use denying all the gin and tonics. Besides, it gave me a chance to text Jackson and let him know exactly what I was bringing home with me. Once we sloshed into the cab, it wasn't hard to convince Lisa to sleep over at my place.

Chapter 12

When we got to my house, Jackson opened the door. He was dressed casually in some baggy sweatpants and a tank top, but I could see Lisa's eyes widen. Nothing is ever casual about Jackson; he looks like a leopard at rest. And nothing sobers a girl faster than being confronted with a man like that.

I told Lisa to wait in the living room; then I pulled Jackson aside and told him my plan. After that it was only a matter of whipping up some guacamole, smoking a little herb, and we were in business. I went to rejoin Lisa.

Lisa and I hung out in the living room, where there were two big couches, including Jackson's couch of exile when the garage was too cold. There were even a few beanbag chairs I had kept around from college. I was glad Jackson had thought to shove the bedding he used behind the couch, so our domestic issues weren't so obvious.

I was also super glad Chelsea was on a sleepover again. I texted her to make sure she was okay and got the impatient *Yes, Mom!* response a few minutes later. She hadn't learned to blow me off yet, though with her growing adolescent attitude, that might happen sooner than later. For now, we were good.

I found myself staring at Lisa. Even with that baggy shirt concealing her unfairly large breasts, she looked like a catch. Her high heels contrasted with her casual top, but they also sealed the deal. Lisa seemed to be crossing her muscular legs a lot. She was restless, perhaps a bit agitated at seeing a hunky guy just when she thought the night's adventures were behind us.

"Did Nick approve this outfit?" I asked her, jokingly. Her face flushed.

"No, he's out of town at a conference," she said.

I smiled at her teasingly.

"What's that look for?" she asked me. "I told you, I've been good lately!"

"I would assume no less!" My chin jutted in the direction of my husband. "Speaking of which, would you like to see Jackson model some swimsuits for us?"

"Swimsuit model?" Lisa asked me, somewhat disbelievingly. "I thought he was in construction."

"Jackson is part of a male swimsuit contest for charity next weekend. It's an annual tradition. Bring home the prize and raise some money for breast cancer."

"Oh, *really*?" She wasn't buying it.

"Yeah, he used to be a stripper in college," I said, trying not to show how proud I was. It was a stupid thing to be proud of.

"But he won't be stripping," I paused, "at the event next week." I waggled my eyebrows. "What do you say, Lisa? We could have Jackson show us his suits, and we can pick out a favorite."

"Yeah, sure!" Lisa said. "I'm not one to turn down a personal male revue." She plopped from one of the couches into the bean bag after pulling it around. I did the same, but not before running to get Jackson away from his computer and into action. The plan was working perfectly.

A few minutes went by as my feelings of deviousness

mounted. *Oh, Corrie, you're about to do a very bad thing* ....

"Okay, Jackson, let's get it going!" I said. I scrolled through our iPod, moving it off "jazz mix" and onto "disco classics." Andy Gibb came on with "I Just Want to Be Your Everything."

"That's the right groove," I said. Lisa cracked up, starting to get into this.

"Jackson, c'mon!" I yelled out.

Jackson turned the hallway corner, wearing a V-neck and swim shorts.

"Woohoo!" we both hollered. This first swimsuit was baggy and loose fitting.

I thought I saw disappointment on Lisa's face. "Take it off!" she said, pointing to Jackson's shirt.

Hips gyrating, Jackson took off his T-shirt. Unlike most of the male species, Jackson was never ashamed to move in front of the ladies. He wasn't a six-pack abs kind of guy, but Jackson did have a powerful build that was pleasing to horny girls like us. "Oh, baby!" Lisa called out. She could see from my happy look I wasn't offended at the fun she was having.

Jackson grabbed a bean bag chair and started humping it a little bit as Lisa cackled.

"Jackson," I scolded, "no beanbag babies. Next outfit!"

The next pair of shorts was even baggier, but at least Jackson kept his shirt off this time. By now, the song had changed. Jackson was swaying to "Funky Town," doing his best to keep the beat. Jackson would never qualify for *Dancing with the Stars*, but he had a certain indefinable something. I could see a flicker of lust on Lisa's face. For the first time, I felt a surge of possessiveness.

"How about something a little snugger," Lisa called out to him. "I wanna see ... those glutes!"

Jackson laughed. "I'll see what I can find!" he said, hip thrusting his way out of the room to our catcalls.

Jackson came out again, ass first, shakin' his booty in a tighter getup as the next song kicked in: "I'm Your Boogie Man," by KC and the Sunshine Band.

"Work it, boogie man!" I called out while Lisa squealed happily. It was great to see her forgetting her troubles; she had helped me do the same on many occasions.

As Jackson worked the beat, his shorts clung to his buns. Then he turned, gyrating his hips. These pants were also pretty baggy in front, but you could see his ropy penis flopping all over the place. I heard Lisa gasp a little bit, no doubt questioning what she was seeing.

"Jackson, look for something tighter!" I said, as he backed out of the room. Donna Summer's "Hot Stuff" kicked in.

"Like a thong," I thought I heard Lisa say under her breath.

And that's exactly what came next. This time, Jackson didn't wear a swimsuit. He busted around the corner in a red thong we had special-ordered for him last Christmas from an online store for well-endowed men. It turned me on so much just to order from it.

"Oh … my … god!" I heard Lisa call out. Jackson is probably about six inches soft, and he wasn't totally soft anymore. He started vigorously humping to the music; you could see his big floppy cock swinging like a pendulum, ominously pushing in our direction.

"Holy shit!" Lisa said, "What a—"

"Work it baby! Show her what you can do!" I encouraged him. Jackson moved his hips sideways, gyrating his way toward us, his cock straining in the red pouch.

"God, Corrie," Lisa whispered, "I had no idea."

"Can he show you a little more?" I asked her, my gin and tonics giving me the boldness I needed.

Lisa just said, "Okay …" as if in a daze, compulsively squeezing her thighs together.

I shut off the disco and kneeled in front of Jackson. "Honey, I want to show my girl what you have to offer," I said, gripping his thickness.

"Sure, baby." Jackson smiled down at me. I pulled his thong down to his ankles and his cock sprung out, almost whacking me in the face.

"Now that's what I call sprung!" I called out and smiled at Lisa. The always-verbal Lisa had nothing to say.

I started jerking Jackson's cock, as if I always did this kind of thing in front of my friends. He was two-thirds hard now, getting thicker and heavier with every stroke. *Baam*! For the first time in a long while, I felt some wetness between my own legs. With Lisa's gaze upon us, I was rediscovering my own husband's cock.

"Oh that's it, that's it, Corrie," Jackson said.

"I want to get him nice and hard so you can see," I told Lisa, turning sideways so I could stroke Jackson with both hands and get him to his hardest point. Jackson never got totally steel-hard, which might have been a problem with a small cock. With his size, it wasn't an issue.

I could tell he was turned on by how his cock was throbbing in my hands. That was another good thing about Jackson. He almost never spurted without a lot of effort on my part, so you could stroke him without losing the moment.

"Wow, Jackson, that's about as hard as I've seen you," I said. It was true. He wasn't sticking straight out, or higher as some of my other lovers had. But Jackson was hard, all right, sticking out at a mean-looking angle. I turned to show Lisa, but she had already moved to the edge of the beanbag for a better view.

Her hand was on her hips; she was clearly fighting the urge to jam her fingers right up her skirt. This was going even better than I'd expected.

"Oh, Lisa, I'm sorry, I'm being so selfish. Why don't you come over here and play with Jackson too?" I said.

Lisa looked at me and said nothing, as if to question my intentions.

"It's okay, I get to have him all the time," I said, doing my utmost to pretend he and I weren't in a rough patch. "C'mon, there's plenty to share." I held Jackson's cock up toward her. Feeling the power it had on my old friend made me squirmier than I'd been in a while. Lisa obediently slid over, almost in a trance.

She kneeled next to me, looking up at Jackson as if worshipping some dark god. I took her right hand and placed it on Jackson's cock, next to mine.

"Oh my god, it's so big in my hand!" Lisa said, her little fingers barely encompassing him.

She started stroking; I moved lower to massage his heavy balls.

"Oh …. careful, Corrie," Jackson moaned. The only time he cums too fast is when his cock and balls are massaged together.

But I had other things in mind.

"Lisa, you go ahead. I want to see how you stroke him." Her eyes showed uncertainty as I fell back into a beanbag chair.

But Lisa's lust got the better of her and she went back to stroking. Soon she was working Jackson with both hands, looking up at him to gauge his reaction to her grip and tempo.

"Oh, Jackson," Lisa said, her brain melting to servitude.

And then, taking us both by surprise, Lisa leaned in and put the head of Jackson's cock into her mouth.

"That's it, baby," Jackson said. "Suck this dick."

Now it was my turn to be shocked, watching my friend Lisa go nuts on my husband right in front of me.

Soon, Lisa was slobbering all over his cock, making crazy sucking sounds, slapping his dick on her face then going back to sucking and stroking.

Falling back on her knees, she practically ripped her own shirt off and undid her bra, tossing it across the room before going back to sucking Jackson's dick as if famished.

Jackson laughed appreciatively. For the first time in months, I needed to get off, I *had* to get off. I feverishly lifted my red dress and stuck my hand down, plunging a couple of fingers into my wetness. *Bang! Oh shit* …. Jackson and I were on a moving train again.

And that was when Jackson took control.

He pushed Lisa off his cock, which she had not succeeded in sucking properly anyhow. He was too thick to deep-throat and she was too worked up to concentrate.

With his most commanding tone, he told Lisa, "Get the rest of your clothes off, slut; you're about to get fucked."

Another jolt surged through me. I figured Lisa would slap Jackson hard for calling her a slut out of nowhere like that. But she looked at me for permission instead. The look was not anger; it was more of a question. I guess seeing my hand frantically working my clit under my dress was all the permission Lisa needed.

Lisa ripped off her skirt and panties with urgency, as if she only had seconds to do so.

She was about to take off her red heels, but Jackson stopped her. "That's it," he said soothingly. "That's a good little slut." That only made Lisa moan and grunt loader. "Yeah, Lisa, let it out. I knew from the second you set foot in this house you'd be slobbering all over my cock." He looked her up and down. "Look at your thighs, Lisa, you're dripping horny!" Jackson said, and it was true. Her discarded red panties were soaked, and her juices were starting to leak down her legs.

Realizing we might have a problem with the light carpet Jackson put in last summer, I ran into the hallway closet and grabbed a sheet.

"Corrie!" Jackson called out. "Can you put that extra sheet on the bed for us? Lisa's gonna need it."

Fuck! I was slippery wet myself. I'd cum a river with just a bit of help. Trembling, I put the extra sheet down in the bedroom, not quite believing what was happening.

By the time I came back out, Jackson was making his move. He picked Lisa up and carried her to the guest bedroom, her ass resting above his dick. I was glad for that. Even with my daughter at a sleepover, this was a bit too much sex for the family living room.

I followed behind. Then I remembered there wasn't a good place to sit in that room. I went back for a beanbag chair and dragged it behind me. In the guest bedroom, things were getting out of hand.

Jackson had his hands on his hips. He pointed toward the bed. "Lisa, lie on that bed now so you can get your pussy fucked!" he said with authority. Lisa jumped onto the bed immediately, spreading her legs wide, compulsively rubbing herself and lost in a slutty daze.

She squirmed with anticipation as he kneeled over her. He pushed her legs wide and slapped his heavy cock down on her, halfway up her belly. With her hips rubbing up against him she looked like such a goddess, albeit a goddess in heat.

Lisa reached up and pulled Jackson to her, trying to guide his face into her pussy. But Jackson pulled away, yanking her to the end of the bed.

"I'm not here to lick pussy," Jackson said indignantly, forcing her legs toward him. "We're here to fuck!"

"But I'm not ready!" Lisa called out, unconvincingly.

"Oh you're ready, slut," Jackson said, working his fingers inside her pussy. "You're wet as hell, and I'm fucking you now!"

Jackson looked over at me, and seeing no obvious protest, he proceeded to jam his cock into her without the care he usually took.

"Owwwww!!" Lisa cried.

But Jackson kept going, mercilessly, raising her thighs up and pushing in further.

"Owwwww!!" Lisa yelled again. "Go slower!"

But she didn't say "stop."

And Jackson didn't stop.

I was so weak-kneed, it was all I could do to hike my skirt up and lie back on that beanbag chair. Neither one noticed me, and I looked on, fascinated. Somehow, this as way more intense than our time with Alicia. Maybe because I was watching a girl get conquered by Jackson for the first time. A friend of mine, no less. And yeah, in my sexual trance, I forgot about condoms yet again. *Don't rub it in.*

"I'm not going slower, I'm going faster!"

And with that, Jackson pounded into Lisa even harder, burying two-thirds of his cock inside her.

"Owwwww!" Lisa yelled, but less convincingly than before, as if pleasure was sneaking in around the pain.

Either way, Jackson wasn't stopping.

The next few minutes were about Lisa's unintelligible screams, somewhere between pain and pleasure.

I could make out a couple of "Oh my gods." In the meantime I was working my pussy like crazy and had already cum a bit, though I could feel a *much* bigger cum building.

It was astonishing to watch Jackson completely take my girlfriend like that—the same exact girl who had swatted so many men down like flies over the years. I watched in rapture, working my wanton pussy in front of them as if we did this every weekend.

Jackson was giving Lisa the fucking of her twenty-something life. But even as he fucked her savagely and seemed so out of control, he really wasn't. I could tell … because he did not try to push his entire cock into her.

Still, he was pounding her hard, expertly stopping and pulling out before hitting bottom then jamming back in. The sound was beautifully obscene, like a massive plunger jamming all the air and water out of her cunt.

"That's it, bitch, cum on me."

OMG. I came like crazy myself, holding my thighs together and shaking sideways. It gets me so hot that Jackson knows girls are about to cum on his cock, even before they realize it. Maybe it's a distant vibration he feels because his thick cock is so firmly tugging the vaginal walls, I don't know. He is a pussy whisperer.

"Your slutty pussy is going to cum all over my cock!" Jackson belted out.

Sure enough, a couple minutes later, she hissed out through the moans and screams, "Oh my god, I think I'm gonna cum …. Keep fucking me like that!!"

Jackson pushed her legs out a bit farther and pounded into her, slowing the pace slightly and focusing on the exact rhythm.

Now even I could see it; we all could. Lisa was working her hips up to him, begging for his cock, but her leg muscles were shaking and giving way. A tremble started in her hips, rippling up and down her body as her arms flailed on the bed, her fingers grasping at the sheets.

"Cummming!!! she screamed.

It was so beautiful to watch her lose control that I forgot to be jealous.

Finally, Lisa's cum slowed down, and Jackson's pace as well. But he kept his dick inside her.

"Oh wow," Lisa said, her arms like noodles against the sheets. "That was just incredible," she mewled, looking over at me happily, as if it was totally normal to see me masturbating casually in front of her, in between orgasms myself. "I've *never* cum from fucking before … ever!" Lisa said gratefully. "Well, not without a little help from my own fingers," she added, touching her clit. "But that," Lisa exhaled as Jackson continued to slowly work her, "*that* was different."

"Oh that's nothing!" Jackson said. "That was just a warm-up cum. Wait till I get my whole dick inside you."

She moaned at that, and Jackson took that as permission to re-insert.

That was when I remembered the condoms, or lack thereof.

"Jackson … condoms!"

Lisa got a petulant look on her face; I could tell she was getting into the thrusting again.

"But Corrie, I'm on the pill," she protested, cupping her breasts and rubbing them together while Jackson worked his way in.

"Nope. Condoms required!" I said.

Fortunately, we still had some condoms around. Truth be told, we never used them, but I got an erotic charge out of buying Magnums from the adolescent clerks at the drug stores. The looks on their faces—especially the girls—were always priceless.

I rummaged through the top dresser drawer and grabbed the Magnum XLs.

"Out, Jackson! Pull it out!"

He reluctantly obeyed, his dick making a sucking sound, causing Lisa to laugh but then whine at his absence.

I kneeled in front of him, but I soon realized his dick was far too wet to put a condom on.

"Jeezus, Lisa, you came all over him!" I teased her, running into the bath to grab a towel as she laughed.

I didn't want to lose the moment. Lisa propped herself up on a pillow, masturbating casually as she watched me work the condom on Jackson's penis. Even this size condom wasn't wide enough to hold him comfortably, but it hadn't broken on us yet.

Once the condom was on, I turned Jackson around. Without a second thought, I started guiding his penis right into her pussy. She didn't protest. Her eyes popped wide as his head entered her, and it was on.

Chapter 13

"FUCK HER BRAINS OUT, Jackson!" I demanded. Though he wasn't able to get his entire dick inside Lisa, he was able to get her into some new positions that caused her to erupt. Her red heels flailed in the air as she screamed bloody murder. Eventually she dug her heels into his back and started fucking him just as hard, lifting her hips straight up off the bed, desperate not to lose his cock as he pulled back. Jackson had heel marks in his back for the next two weeks—to give you some idea of her fucking wanton urgency.

The next hour or so is a blur. I remember taking off my clothes with some urgency, plopping back down, and working myself to a monster orgasm while Lisa gripped the sheets for dear life.

The hottest point came when Lisa complained, "Ouch! I can't take all of you yet."

With a look of mild irritation, Jackson picked her right up off the bed, his big penis still inside her. Then he stood, raising her up and forcing her down on his dick with her own weight.

"Oh my god!" and then, "You're so much bigger than Nick! That feels so fucking good!!"

As Lisa screamed with pleasure, I started casually working my clit again. Maybe I wasn't done yet.

"You're a slut for my cock!" Jackson said.

"Oh god, I am—"

"Who fucks you better, me or him?"

"Oh god, you do!!"

With that, Lisa started cumming so hard Jackson had to sit on the mattress to stabilize her. Then he flung her down, pulled his cock out, and quickly started fingering her. That could only mean one thing.

"C'mon!" he called out. "C'mon!"

Lisa started squirting all over Jackson's hands and all over the end of the bed.

"Oh, shit!!" Lisa called out.

Why did all the girls get to squirt but me? Judging by Lisa's reaction, she was new to squirting also. After she came, she kept whimpering and mewling, her thighs vibrating as she tentatively explored herself, examining her own condition.

Seeing my old bestie cum like that was it for me. Soon I was clamping down on my hand so hard, it felt like I might crush it with my thighs.

Lisa, meanwhile, was a puddle on the bed, half woman, half orgasm.

"Oh god, Jackson," Lisa cooed. "I have *never* been fucked like that."

Jackson smiled as he pulled the condom off with a loud snap, his dick still hard.

"Corrie, I had no idea," Lisa said.

"No idea what?" I teased her.

"No idea there were dicks that big, dicks that could be—"

"Used so well?"

"Oh yeah," Lisa said. "That was perfect."

And that was when it happened. Seeing Lisa so happy, so utterly fulfilled, then flashing back to the happy yells of Alicia … a voice of bizarre reason popped into my head:

Jackson is right: he WAS born to please women.
And you'd be ridiculously selfish to keep him to yourself.

When Jackson had said this exact thing before, I'd reacted with anger, then denial. This time, the thought lingered. I didn't yet realize all the implications, but one thing I did know: I took a twisted, less than admirable pleasure in disrupting Lisa's own relationship.

And we disrupted it quite a bit further.

My favorite part of that first night was Lisa and me kneeling next to each other, looking up in lust while we worked Jackson's cock with our hands, determined to make him cum. Trying to make Jackson cum made my pussy so wet, thinking about all the small, shy dicks that had spurted so quickly in my hand or pussy.

"Lisa, keep jacking him off, do it hard!" I commanded. Meantime, I started working Jackson's balls, and he didn't tell me to stop. That meant he was done holding out. He was ready to let go.

I could hear him moaning and breathing heavily. It was on!

"Cum for your sluts, Jackson!" I yelled at him. I felt his body give that telltale tremble and did a mean thing: I aimed his dick toward Lisa.

Jackson bucked and came—rope after rope, about six in rapid succession, then three more after he slowed down. In all the years of jerking him off, I'd never seen him cum as much as that.

"Oh my god," Lisa said, "you are such a man!!" She had cum all over her, and she wasn't even pissed at me. Unlike what the pornos would have you believe, it's not fun to get so much cum on you. Honestly, I'd prefer to avoid it.

Lisa was still so turned on, I let her get in the shower with him to wash him off. A few minutes later, I actually had to go in there and prevent them from fucking in the shower.

"Condoms!" I yelled out, without offering one.

They took their hands off each other, Lisa with reluctance.

I got her tucked into the couch for sleeping before she could make any more trouble. Lisa still snored like a sailor, but that was fine by me—easier to keep tabs on her that way.

In the morning, Lisa was gone. She left a very simple note on the back of a restaurant coaster, with a big heart around it and an "xoxo" underneath. "THANK YOU BOTH! —Lisa."

We still have the coaster. It's always funny when someone turns it upside down and asks what it means.

Chapter 14

THAT EPISODE WITH LISA ushered in a radically different sexual mood between Jackson and myself.

I still wasn't right emotionally. But Jackson was too happy that our sex life was finally clicking to worry about that. Suddenly, it felt like right after we'd met—we couldn't keep our paws off each other. Except this time we had to work to avoid having sex openly when our daughter was around. She must have heard noises, but her smiles in the morning seemed happy. She was definitely glad Jackson wasn't sleeping in the garage anymore. Most nights he wasn't on the couch either.

But if I wasn't right emotionally, I was absolutely all right sexually. Jackson and I were fucking constantly. I was late to work twice because I needed an extra fuck in the morning—and that wasn't like me. It didn't help me with my boss much, but I'm about to get to that.

Another clue to my marital riddle appeared the following weekend. Thank god it was another sleepover for Chelsea, because Jackson was really nailing me to the wall. The bed board was actually whacking the wall hard enough to leave a mark, but I didn't care.

I just wanted to be fucked into oblivion. Post-orgasm, Jackson and I were casually fucking. I leaned up on my elbows, fascinated as always to see how his thickness pulled my lips out of my pussy. That tug always felt soooo good.

"Oh, Jackson, thank you for taking such good care of my pussy."

"Anything for you, Alpha Phi." Jackson always liked to reference my former sorority. I think he still got off on thinking of some of the havoc he once wreaked on sorority girls.

"It's good I didn't know you in college," I said, wrapping my legs around him and pulling him closer, savoring the fullness.

"Why?" he said.

"I'm not sure I would have graduated. You would have been up in my room and all up in my pussy out all day long."

"Ah, but would you have shared me with your roommate?" Jackson asked.

"No!" I said instantly. But then I added, "Well, maybe."

I hadn't told him yet. But now I did.

"Oh, Jackson, I'm sorry I tried to keep you to myself." I sighed. "You're right," I added, letting the fullness of him sink in. "You *were* born to fuck."

I had been fighting this truth for months … for years. No, from the first time I met him. And now I'd said it. *So ridiculous, but so obvious. And so true.*

"I'm not going to make you stay faithful anymore. I know the other girls will never leave you alone. And Jackson … they deserve to be feel as good as you can make them feel."

He leaned forward and kissed me, but it was not a tender fairytale kiss. For him, it was a moment of victory. For me, it a moment of relief. I felt like a bizarre marital weight had been lifted from my shoulders.

"It's about time you said it," Jackson said. "I tried to warn you."

"I know you did," I said, savoring his slow grind.

"The truth is, I've let you off easy," Jackson said.

What the fuck was he talking about?

But with his dick moving in rhythmic circles and spreading heat across my midsection, it was hard to be mad.

Nevertheless, I asked him angrily, "What do you mean?"

"The fact is I own this pussy," he said. "I've owned this pussy ever since the first night we met."

No man had *ever* spoken to me like this!

"I respected your anger, but now I realize it was a mistake," he said, circling and thrusting, circling and thrusting. "I own this pussy, and from now on, I call the shots."

I felt *so mad*, so disrespected, and ... so *fucking horny*.

Jackson had picked up the pace while I was freaking out.

He was pounding me hard now, but instead of resisting, I was thrusting my hips up to meet him, desperate for his cock.

"Who owns this pussy?" Jackson yelled out.

I just fucked him harder, and I felt that subtle scratching of a deep itch, that first sign of a quaking vaginal orgasm, one that wouldn't burst out of me for a few more minutes. A trickle to a stream to a goddamn river.

"Who owns this pussy?" Jackson demanded. And then, slamming my hips into him, I surrendered.

"Oh god, Jackson, you do! You've always owned this pussy!"

"That's right, you fucking slut! Give me your pussy, give it to me hard. Show me how bad you want it!!"

And with that, he mostly stopped thrusting, standing firm and letting me do the work as I primitively thrust my cunt at him, determined to claim my orgasm.

God, I couldn't believe how much this turned me on. He was putting me in my place, and I had never needed anything so badly.

"That's it, you fucking slut, you're a whore for my cock!"

"Oh god yes, I'm such a slut for your big dick! Make my pussy cum, Jackson!"

He held my hips to his body with an iron grip as I had a crazy cum all over his dick, my hips releasing layers of tension I didn't even know I had.

I had never cried out of lust before, but I did now.

And it wasn't over.

After Jackson let my hips down on the bed, he forced himself deep inside me again.

"Jackson, wait!" We always took it slow after a big cum, allowing my pussy to regroup and my tender clit to recover.

"No!" Jackson said. "You were about to squirt! I'm gonna make you squirt!"

"I've never squirted," I told him … feeling annoyed and more than a bit sore.

"You're going to squirt, I can tell!" Jackson laughed and pushed my legs back, deepening the angle.

"You don't know that!" I said, starting to feel pleasure mixed with that sore irritability.

"I can feel it!" Jackson said. "I can feel you vibrating."

I couldn't feel it, but I could tell I was going to have another decent cum if he fucked me, so I went along with it.

Jackson wasn't pounding too hard, but he was precisely pushing and withdrawing. Same angle, same thrust. I was fucking him back, not super hard, more curious than anything.

And then I felt something. Just a little something, but an inkling, a tingle that started in my neck and traveled down my spine into my pelvic bone.

"Oh, I'm about to make you squirt, Corrie!" He was smiling and laughing, happy to prove himself. I hated his arrogance and loved it completely.

"Just like I made Donna squirt!"

"Donna? Donna?!"

Donna was an old friend I had become estranged from due to her devout Mormonism.

"You fucked Donna?"

"Yeah! She squirted all over me like a slut!" Jackson cackled.

In my mind I flashed to Donna, a big-boned girl who pretended sex was only for man and wife, a six-foot-tall athlete who would utterly intimidate most men.

Then all these women flashed into my mind, the ones Jackson had told me about, others he hadn't, older married women he fucked while barely a man, all these women gratefully cumming all over him while their boyfriends and husbands and wannabe boyfriends stroked their little dicks somewhere else and prayed that something wasn't wrong, or maybe that something was, something deep, deep down ....

And that was it. The floodgates opened. It was slow motion, but I remember Jackson pulling me to him as rivers of fluid spurted out of my pussy, wave after wave. It was a huge release, beyond any kind of a cum, as if years of stress were balled up and then exhaled in a surge of pleasure. It was the best feeling I'd ever had.

"You squirted!" Jackson said, forced to withdraw his cock as my pussy literally expelled him with the force of its fluids.

"Good girl," he said.

I don't remember exactly what happened next. I think I babbled to him about everything inside my strange, addicted heart. Then we tapered off. Jackson left me to get a drink— that much I recall. I remember lying in bed, thinking that my marriage had fundamentally changed.

He owns you now.

But ... I have never been owned in my life, by any man! Certainly not in the bedroom.

Doesn't matter ... he owns your pussy. And therefore, he owns you.

But ... this isn't good! This gives him too much power.

Maybe so, but it's true. So live with it. Find your power elsewhere.

Chapter 15

T HE FOLLOWING DAYS WERE interesting, to say the least. I expected Jackson to exert his newfound power over me. If he had demanded I quit my job and scrub the floors all day for him, I would have complied.

But he didn't. Jackson wasn't a book-smart guy, but he could play these notes. Outside of the bedroom, he continued to pretend I was the one with the final word. That had a way of calming me down—making me feel like I hadn't surrendered too much.

But we both knew. Deep down, we knew. He had control now. And I hated it … except that I loved it. Well, my pussy loved it, anyway. Jackson now took me whenever he wanted. One morning, he simply fucked me as I was walking toward the front door. He bent me over the kitchen counter and violently fucked my pussy with my suit skirt hiked up as I clutched my coffee thermos. I screamed and screamed, confessing my sluttitude and how deep it went.

But when the sex was done and my makeup hastily reapplied, it was back to the domestic façade of mutual respect.

You might be thinking, *Well, it was a strange way to fix your marriage, Corrie, but at least it worked.* Alas, not so much. Aside from the persistence of lust, I didn't feel much of anything. My sex life was not only reawakened, it was fundamentally transformed. I wanted Jackson like a schoolgirl; I came home from work with my panties already damp. All I could think about in every meeting and conference call was him bending me over and taking me. Sometimes I even masturbated in the bathroom stall on the top floor of our building.

It was only in a quiet moment, like watching my daughter trying her first Kung Fu moves in the backyard, that I realized something was amiss. Feelings of normal momhood would surge through me, and my ice would crack—but only temporarily. The next morning Jackson would have me bent over any chair he felt like fucking me on. Was I headed down a road of total depravity, never to return?

Aside from quiet moments with Chelsea, I was a full-time slut. I was living in a bunch of outtakes from *Fifty Shades of Grey*. Ecstasy without soul.

Jackson didn't lord his victory over me. Aside from the moments of animal conquest, he seemed to almost empathize, like he understood me somehow.

So when Lisa started texting him behind my back, he didn't keep it from me like he could have. He didn't go over and fuck her like he could have. He didn't tell me he was going to fuck her senseless and dare me to stop him.

No, he did none of those things, though he could have done them all, and I wouldn't have lifted a finger. Instead, he did something different: he got Lisa on the line and handed me the phone.

Lisa was surprised.

"Oh, hi …" she said, pretending it was normal to be texting and calling my husband.

"Lisa, I think you'd better come over."

"Oh … okay." She was clearly reluctant.

"Jackson and I would like to … see you."

She paused, but I knew she couldn't resist. We made a plan and hung up.

"Jackson!" I called out to him. He was back in the garage again, fixing a busted gutter.

"Yes, honey!" he called out.

"Jackson, Lisa is coming over. I want you to be gone before she gets here."

"No problem," he said.

"And then I want you to come back over when I text you and fuck her till she can't finish a sentence," I said.

Jackson laughed but said, "Okay, no problem."

A few minutes later, Jackson took off on his motorbike. It was an early spring day, finally warm enough for riding.

I washed the dishes, as if that was the task you really needed to get done before your good friend came over to fuck your husband.

As I over-scrubbed each dish, I thought about how annoyed I was that Lisa had gone behind my back to get to Jackson. But I didn't feel distrust toward Jackson anymore.

Now that he controls you, he has no reason to lie.

It was true, and what's more, it solved a very difficult problem between us—a problem no amount of heart-to-heart talks had ever been able to fix.

But Lisa's sneakiness still bugged me. She came in, looking a little sheepish. But beyond that, determined. I guess there was no turning back for her either.

I sat her down on the couch, offering only ice water. I didn't want her to feel too relaxed yet.

"So, Lisa, you've been calling Jackson a time or two, huh?"

Lisa crossed her legs. I couldn't help but notice those telltale red heels, clicking against each other nervously.

"Yeah, my car's been giving me trouble, and I needed some advice on—"

"Oh Lisa, just spare me." I rolled my eyes. "I know why you were calling him."

Lisa's face turned reddish brown in anger and embarrassment, but she didn't deny it.

What I did next surprised even me. I set my water down, went over to where Lisa was sitting, and straddled her.

"Oh my god, Corrie …. What are you doing?"

I kissed her, and not too tenderly either.

Her eyes popped wide, but I could feel her kissing me back.

I pushed her down on the couch, swinging my leg over hers as if I dominated girls all the time.

Then I leaned over. "Lisa, I know you want to fuck Jackson again." Not waiting for a reply, I worked my fingers right down under her little "fuck me" skirt and found my way toward her sticky slit.

"Ohhhhh," was all she could say.

"Oh yeah, your pussy is already all wet. You were thinking about Jackson fucking you all day, now weren't you?"

"Yes," Lisa said helplessly, thighs greedy against my fingers.

"Well, Lisa, guess what? I have some good news for you. I've decided that Jackson is too good a fuck to keep to myself. So I'm going to let you fuck him again, but under a couple of conditions." I worked another finger up and down her slit and poked one gently inside.

She was in no position to argue, but asked anyway, "What conditions?"

"Well, first off, if you ever want to fuck Jackson again, you have to go through me. Think of me as Jackson's pimp; you make appointments. You *never* go around me. And you *never* fuck him when I'm not there." I put my weight on her body for emphasis. I thought I saw a quick flash of fear in her eyes. Was I that crazy? "Not unless I say so," I continued, rotating my hand against her clit. I'd been with a couple of girls in college and knew how to handle a girl like Lisa.

"Okay," said Lisa expectantly.

"But there's another condition," I said.

"Anything!" Lisa moaned as my fingers found her spots …. Now we were getting somewhere.

"I want you to confess how much better he is than Nick."

Lisa blushed.

"I mean it, Lisa!" I said, pulling my fingers out of her as she exhaled.

Lisa looked defeated. But maybe a little relieved too. "Oh god yeah, he fucks me so much better," she said.

"That's right," I said, putting my fingers back inside to encourage her.

"I've never cum so much or so hard in my life," she continued, warming to the subject. It's like he can feel what my body needs before I even know it."

"And then he gives it to you exactly the way a slut dreams it can be, right?"

"Oh god, yes!" Lisa said. "He makes me feel like such a woman. Oh god, I need it so bad!" she cried. I could feel her body responding as I worked the inner walls of her pussy, her body pulsing under my hand.

"And what else, Lisa, what else?"

"I ..." she drew the word out.

"Lisa, just say it, or Jackson won't be fucking you again."

She was too worked up to hold back now. "His dick is just so much bigger!!"

"That's right, Lisa. Just admit how good it feels. There's no shame in being a slut for Jackson."

"It feels so much better inside me!" she said. "Size shouldn't matter this much!" she groaned. "I mean I've never, *ever* cum from intercourse, much less squirted on a cock!"

"Have you tried to fuck Nick since you were with Jackson?" I asked, putting my weight back down on her firmly to make sure she knew I expected the truth.

"Yes," she said, crestfallen. "I tried..." she continued.

"But ..." I said, helping her along.

"I could barely feel anything," she confessed.

I started working her clit with ferocity, sensing she was getting to a fever point.

"He felt so little compared to Jackson," she said, desperate to cum. "And he didn't …."

"What, Lisa?"

"He didn't know what to do to make me his. Jackson, he just … conquered me."

"That's better!" I said approvingly. "Tell me why you're here today, Lisa, then we'll make that pussy cum, get it nice and warmed up for Jackson."

"I'm here to get fucked by a real man!" Lisa said.

"That's right," I said. "You need it so bad you will cheat on Nick whenever Jackson snaps his fingers."

"Oh god, yes!" Lisa yelled out.

"Who owns your pussy, Lisa?"

"Jackson does … Jaaaackson does …." She was starting to lose it, and to be honest, I was too. My husband has one millionth the wealth of Donald Trump, but I ask you, who is the more powerful man? He didn't just have me, he had my friend ready to cheat whenever he snapped his fingers. And it didn't stop there. My pussy was tingling and steaming.

Lisa wasn't faring any better. A little more friction and it would be all over for her; she was putty in my hands, humping wildly against me, cumming like crazy.

I wished I had a big thick penis like Jackson. I would have spread her immediately and put it in her.

But that would happen soon enough. Thirty minutes later, Jackson's motorbike sputtered its arrival. In another ten, he was fucking Lisa good.

"Oh my god, Jackson, put it in me, I want to feel it!" Lisa pleaded, and they were off, her ass wiggling in the air as he got behind and owned her.

I even let her watch me and Jackson fuck when she needed a rest. It was hot to watch Lisa work her clit with abandon while I rode Jackson until I shook. I even showed her how I could take Jackson all the way in a couple of positions, letting him slam into me like he couldn't with her; she still couldn't take the last inch or so of his big dick. The cums were amazing.

I let her put the condoms on Jackson; it was seriously hot to watch her shyly coax that condom over his big dick. She got such a big kick out of opening a Magnum XL condom wrapper, she asked me to take a picture of her doing it. I hoped Nick wouldn't check her phone.

Chapter 16

THIS ARRANGEMENT WENT ON for a month, with Lisa texting me almost every day—nasty, hot texts. I would make her confess over and over exactly why she wanted Jackson, and what she wanted to do with him.

I didn't let her fuck Jackson nearly as often as she would have liked. It required planning to get our daughter out of the house, and we couldn't just leave Chelsea alone while we played sex games.

When I finally felt an emotion rock through me, it wasn't a happy one. It was sparked by Jackson and Lisa getting ready for their tenth fuck session. "God, I think you've ruined me for my boyfriend," Lisa said admiringly, watching Jackson's thick cock twitch and rise in her hand, getting him ready for his condom.

Now it was Lisa who wanted to skip the oral sex and get straight to the fucking. Her pussy was *so* ready on the days she saw Jackson.

And that was starting to worry me. But the deception and the odd arrangements didn't bother Lisa one bit. She was feeling triumphant, because after their fifth fuck session, she could finally take Jackson's cock all the way. Now he could fuck her at a whole new pain/pleasure threshold.

But the more Lisa wanted Jackson's cock, the more he teased her and made her beg for it.

"No fair!" Lisa cried out as she thrust her hips higher, searching for the head of his cock. Jackson laughed as he slapped his cock loudly on her stomach, just out of reach of her pussy.

Lisa watched him intensely, fiddling with her clit while I worked to get the condom over the head and onto the rest of his cock. With that, Jackson had his cockhead up against her, and then came that gratifying "plop" when it went inside her. Lisa immediately started fucking him; she was desperate to start cumming.

"What's wrong, Lisa? Nick not looking after you?" I teased. Lisa put me on ignore and looked up to Jackson with urgency.

"Take it slow, baby," Jackson said, holding her hips down, clearly enjoying the look of surprise/fear/awe on the face of this woman who had men chasing her from dawn to dusk. *Like a virgin*, indeed.

Jackson had a deliciously savage way of making each time just like the first. He knew when to be tender, and just how many lines to cross. Somehow he could straddle that improbable fence between gentleman and ruthless orgasm taker. If only more men knew that secret!

Lisa propped herself up, eager to see how much of Jackson's cock she could take.

"Give me the whole thing!" Lisa implored.

"Patience, my little slut, patience," I said, taking Jackson's lines for my own. "That's it," I hissed into her ear. "Just relax into it; it's always a bit of a struggle at first."

But it wasn't too much of a struggle. Lisa didn't even seem to feel pain as he slowly but decisively bottomed out, holding her there as the first precums started rippling through her legs.

"Jackson, wow," Lisa said, "I can really take it now … I can take all of that big cock!"

Now Jackson was done with gentle fucking. He started pounding into Lisa with no further precautions, working his way up to that vigorous pace that brought the husband-betraying sensations.

"Oh damn … damn … you feel so good inside me!" Lisa cried.

As he accelerated his thrusts, Lisa bucked more and more. She was cumming continuously, releasing the pleasure in waves. Although she had discarded her heels long ago—Jackson was sick of the souvenirs they left on this back—she still banged her bare heels and flailed on him with her fists like a madwoman.

That's when Jackson took complete control, really working her over.

"Fuck, fuck!" Lisa reached around Jackson and pulled his ass into her. Jackson didn't have to fuck too spastically to make pussies cum. That meant he could balance speed with power and rhythm, in and out, *in* and *out*.

Lisa was starting to move toward a big Cum—a capital C kind of Cum—trembling and bucking. "Oh, I'm cummming!! Fuck that feels good," she cried as she gave her pussy to Jackson once again.

"How does it feel to have a real cock inside you?" Jackson taunted her.

"Oh fuck, it feels so incredible! God, I need your dick so bad!!" Lisa's words became unintelligible, happy/lusty grunts. Meanwhile, my own pussy was squirming for attention. *Is that what I was like when I finally got used to taking Jackson's cock all the way?* I wasn't sure, but I could remember how I felt afterward. Fucked out, empty/full, sore, and obsessed with getting him inside me again.

Just like it was for Lisa, it was for me. I thought about it when I was jogging; I thought about it when I was presenting to clients. And I definitely thought about it when men unsuccessfully hit on me or shied away.

I can remember grabbing Jackson's cock in public, and whenever I could, servicing him in some way, completely out of control, sucking him when there was no time to fuck—anything to worship his cock. I even sucked him in my best friend's living room after sending her out for beers, not caring who would walk in on us, almost hoping she would. *Ah, to be young again!*

Lisa finally got out a semi-coherent thought, "Harder, you son of a bitch!" she screamed as Jackson pounded her, her bare heels imploring. By this time, I had already masturbated to a fierce orgasm. As I went to wash up, I heard the perky sounds of her orgasm. Is there a lovelier sound than a woman cumming? When I came back ten minutes later, Lisa had cleaned up and was soul-kissing Jackson.

I had felt jealousy before, watching them fuck, but it was more of a blast of arousal. *This* felt threatening. It wasn't as if Lisa could take Jackson away from me, but I was unsettled. Jackson had an advantage with her: she would be incredibly low maintenance compared to me, and that would be her pitch to him. Or something like that.

Judging from those soulful kisses, I wondered if actual feelings were building between them. That was *not* okay. After Lisa left that day, it occurred to me that Jackson and I hadn't actually made love in a long time—that tender lovemaking you do with someone whose flaws you accept. Lisa, on the other hand, seemed able to let her tenderness show. She was willing to give him *waaay* more than her pussy. I, on the other hand, was still blocked. That scared me.

After she got dressed, I let Lisa know she would no longer be fucking Jackson. The shocked, enraged look on her face told me everything I needed to know. The door slammed behind her, and that was all I heard from Lisa for a few months. I thought she was ridiculous giving me the silent treatment after

I'd let her fuck my husband again and again, but so it goes.

"What got into you?" Jackson asked a bit playfully as we sat together at the kitchen table, coffee brewing.

"I don't know," I said. "I guess I didn't like the way she was looking at you. It seemed like she was forgetting you were my husband."

Jackson wasn't mad about it. He was biding his time. He knew my cunt better than I did, dammit.

I told myself there wouldn't be a next time, at least for a while … and maybe ever. I needed to believe Jackson and I had something he couldn't find elsewhere. *Until we make love, I can't let him be with other women.* But try as I might, kissing Jackson didn't usher in the lovemaking. It was like kissing a sexy male companion. Fashion, not feeling.

I was tormented by the thought of another woman stealing Jackson out from under me. Our sex life started to diminish in intensity again. If I was an addict, I needed a fix.

The hell with that. I was determined to hold off until my obsessive urges went away.

But that didn't happen. It all came to a diabolical head instead.

Chapter 17

For the last six months, my regional office had been terrorized by my new boss, Allen. Allen was everything you don't want in a boss: he made tireless demands and enforced an inconsistent set of rules. He promoted a male colleague above me who had two years less experience and a forty percent lower sales record over the year. I thought that tying my work to actual sales would give me more power internally ... but evidently not with Allen at the helm.

Allen was a skinny little motherfucker, the kind who wore wire-framed glasses to look hipster cool even while he bossed you around. Allen was an Internet smarty pants, super into marathon running when he wasn't acting like a tool at work. You know the type: the holier-than-though, change-into-gym-gear-and-shower-after-lunch type, too fitness obsessed to have a regular meal with his co-workers. Protein shakes and performance reviews. And a sexist jerk to boot, but way too clever to admit it.

When I confronted Allen about the promotion, he said, without skipping a beat, "If you're not happy here, we have an opening in Omaha." What an ass—always pretending he was in complete control, always ready with a cocky comeback. Jackson offered to show up at my job and beat on him, and I was half-worried he might actually do it. I had enough issues on the home front without dreading my workdays. Something had to change.

I tried to sway Allen with my sexuality, just to see if I could crack him. I bought some sexy new outfits. Yes, the pencil skirts that clung to my hips, but also the plunging necklines. Aside from one time when I was presenting over him on the whiteboard, I couldn't get Allen to flinch. It was like he looked through me, or saw me as asexual. *Grrr* ....

One Friday night, I found myself at a "girls' night out" bitch session masquerading as happy hour. Once the drinks started flowing, we went after it. We were making so much noise at TGIF, they moved us to a private room. We started comparing notes on Allen, sharing tales of our tedious encounters.

Aside from the story of how he'd promoted my colleague Randy over me—well within his discretion—we couldn't dredge up much dirt on Allen. He was squeaky clean all right.

One lady, Gretchen, had the misfortune of following Allen around the country. As his executive assistant in three different regions, Gretchen had worked with him the longest.

"Gretchen, didn't he ever make a pass at one of the interns?" I asked hopefully.

"No ... dammit!" Gretchen said. One course away from her MBA, Gretchen was busy plotting to get out from under Allen the Taskmaster. The prospect of greener pastures was probably the only thing keeping her from a meltdown.

"But if he could fuck them with his eyes, we'd have him!" Gretchen said. "Violet, he's stared at your ass so hard I thought he was going to pop a tent," Gretchen said.

Ahh, so he did stare at someone. That was a start!

"Ewwwww!" Violet said. Violet was our college intern, one of those young, spitfire women too confident to know what she was in for. Or maybe she would just bend the world to her will. Violet had one too many tattoos for my liking, but I kept my lecture about career-limiting body art to myself; I enjoyed her company too much. Besides, I always hated it when older women lectured me about my future back in the day.

"I hate the thought of him working me over!" Violet yelled out, squirming as if she'd eaten a slippery raw oyster. We all laughed at her predicament.

"If I catch him doing it …" Violet threatened.

"Oh, he's nailed you from behind many times!" teased Jeannie, a middle-aged battle horse who went to just enough aerobics classes to keep herself in that middle-aged sexy zone. A bit too much makeup for my taste, but Jeannie had a heart of gold. Not to mention all the times she'd saved me with her PowerPoint wizardry.

We burst out laughing at the miserable look on Violet's face.

"It's not all bad," Gretchen teased. "Maybe you can be the first intern to get Allen to spread 'em!"

"Ewwwww!" Violet said again. "He's so skinny, I'd break him in half!" Violet was a big athletic hipper like me. We laughed.

"Give it a shot. I hear there's a position open … above Corrie!" Jeannie cackled. I gave Jeannie a little slap on the behind for that one—not a hard slap, but the sound sent everyone but Jeannie into another gale of laughter.

"Besides, I'll bet he has a tiny penis!" Violet said.

And the mockery continued.

"You know what the worst thing is?" Gretchen blurted out.

"What?"

"His wife, Sirenna—she's so damn hot. He does not deserve a woman like her."

"No!" we all said.

"Maybe he *is* packing!" Jeannie said.

A pause … then, in unison: "No!!" we all agreed, or at least hoped.

"When he comes out in those Lycra shorts, there isn't much to see," said Violet.

"You mean you *look*?" said Gretchen, indignant.

"Maybe she's getting something on the side," Jeannie said.

The other girls laughed, but I didn't. Realizing that she had touched a sore spot, Jeannie said, "Sorry, Corrie." The group grew quiet. The other girls knew about my troubles with Jackson, at least the part about him cheating.

Someone eased the conversation into safer territory. I tried to move on, but for some reason the comment stuck. I left the ladies in their gaggle fifteen minutes later and summoned an Uber.

On the ride home, something odd occurred to me. I thought back to a support group I had attended for about a month. It was for women whose husbands had been unfaithful. To be honest, the group hadn't given me much comfort. I got way more catharsis from the Alicia and Brad Show.

There had been a woman in the group—a striking blonde, the kind of woman who makes you wonder why men invariably mess up the best things in their lives. She was a model type, blonde as all get out, except instead of skinny model hips, she had pin-up girl, hourglass hips like mine. Her breasts were perfect, hanging in the air, taunting women like me who were torn between accepting our smaller breasts and going for unnatural-looking boob jobs. Though I would never get a boob job, this girl had the rare ability to make me think twice about it.

Listening to her made me horny as hell. This woman's name was Sirenna. Now, we don't live in a super small town, but how many Sirennas do you know?

I found myself thinking about Sirenna, remembering some of the things she'd said. That her husband had cheated on her a couple years past. That she was not unhappy in her marriage but worried about her own capacity for cheating and revenge.

Sirenna never had the arrogance to say it in our group, but men had to hit on her a lot. Yet up until that point, she had toed the line. But with "our flat-lined sex life," as she put it, and a disappointing lack of intimacy, how long would that last? She wasn't sure.

One group meeting, she was actually driven to tears. Unlike Jackson, Sirenna's husband hadn't been patient with her. It seemed like he gave her a fixed amount of time, then expected forgiveness. *It had to be the same woman, had to be!* The couch sucked me in. I crashed with late night TV scrolling by, my head on Jackson's lap, pondering coincidences.

At some point I woke up, chilled from a cool fall night. I stumbled into my bed, wrapping the comforter around me selfishly; I always claimed our blankets during the night after Jackson feel asleep. While I slept, evil threads connected. Watching the sun rise under the coziest quilt we had, I began to concoct a devious plan.

I went and woke Jackson, who had fallen asleep on the couch, even though I'd long since welcomed him back into the bedroom. He was playing his cards expertly, and that meant respecting my space to a fault. That is, when he wasn't taking me sexually.

"What is it?" he said, concerned by my intent stare.

"Honey, I need your help."

"Sure ... anything."

"I need you to seduce a woman for me ... at least I think I do."

Chapter 18

I TOLD JACKSON THE plan.

It's not as hard to do these things as you might think. Which is a bit scary, I guess. Catfish is for real.

It wasn't hard to figure out where Sirenna hung out.

It wasn't hard to get my eager-to-fix-our-marriage husband involved in my plot.

It wasn't hard for him to join the gym and the aerobics class she was in.

It wasn't hard for him to make small talk with her and get to be pals.

A month later, Sirenna and Jackson were chummy. Oh, and she said her husband's name was "Allen." *Bingo*.

One week after that, he was making her scream.

Okay, so that last part wasn't easy. Most men either shy away from hot girls or go for broke, with one over-the-top approach. Jackson, however, knows that girls need some warming up.

When you are a hulking guy like Jackson who can intimidate with his bulk, it's all the more disarming when you prove to be a funny and gentle companion. Most guys think girls want tough and stoic, but what really gets them is danger and mystery wrapped in debonair charm. Once you make the girl feel both hot and safe to explore her flirty ways, you step back and let her do the rest—go down a path you cleverly set her on. That's how Jackson describes it to me, anyway. Something emanates from Jackson that forces a woman's hand, yet she thinks he is taking the lead. It's fucking twisted.

That's where most men go wrong. Even when they do succeed in establishing a witty rapport, they push ahead, sending out whiffs of desperation, or they pull back, trying to act indifferent … and nothing happens. Refusing to accept this ego-denying reality, the man pushes ahead again … and gets rebuffed in ways subtle or direct.

If Jackson pulls back and the girl doesn't pursue, he doesn't sweat it. He moves on to the next girl. He knows the odds will favor him sooner than later. Besides, if he manages to fuck one of her friends, she might come back around. During the flirtation, Jackson acts thoughtful, interested, and considerate, but he makes a point of dropping little hints about his virility.

Often these are visual cues, like showing up to an aerobics class in spandex, or getting a bit of a hard-on during a flirty moment. Now and again, he might allude to sex in a way that shows he has experience—nothing outrageous, but enough for a girl to get a distinct feeling that this very nice man is also a *man*.

Of course, when Jackson is impatient or horny, he just tells a girl bluntly what he wants. He's been laid more than a few times by simply having a drink with a hottie and saying, "I want to fuck your brains out with my big dick," or something equally direct.

It's not his most successful technique in terms of percentages, but it works more often than you'd think. There are plenty of girls who love skipping the small talk and the difficulty of gauging what the man is after. Add to that a guaranteed "big cock encounter," and Jackson often finds this is the most effective way to get laid quickly.

But with Sirenna, he didn't want to risk the direct approach. She seemed like too much of a married lady, used to discretion and decorum. So I asked him to charm her into a casual friendship.

We executed "Operation Sirenna" to perfection. After Jackson met Sirenna at her gym, we compared notes to make sure she was a match. Leggy blonde with old school sex appeal? Check. Large-but-not-huge tits, nearly six feet tall? Check.

Yeah, we deceived Sirenna. I had *not* deceived Jackson, however. He knew she was my boss's wife. Yes, he was worried this scheme might blow up, but I wasn't having any. There were plenty of jobs out there.

Jackson was blinded by his desire to somehow eradicate my discontent. He had broken me down sexually, but he had no idea how to fix my heart.

You probably want to know how the seduction happened. Jackson simply adjusted his work schedule around Sirenna's aerobics class. I got a kick out of watching him shimmy his landscaping pants over his Lycra workout shorts in the morning.

Under normal circumstances, I didn't like him wearing those shorts; they were a billboard for his cock, all bunched up in that cramped space. It looked like he was stuffing his pants.

I hated thinking about the ladies in the class flirting shamelessly with Jackson. He played it down afterward, but there must have been some heavy estrogen in there. Typically about twenty people showed up; Jackson was one of three or so guys who made a regular appearance.

It wasn't hard for him to strike up a conversation with Sirenna. One day, he offered her a Kind bar when she was complaining to friends about leaving her lunch at home. The next week, he asked her to teach him a leg stretch before class, claiming a hamstring issue.

After each class, I'd ask Jackson, "Did you get her number?"

And he's say something like, "Not yet, baby. Let me do my thing."

Jackson was using a seduction tactic he called "The Smooth." The Smooth was a long game tactic that got the woman to warm up to him as both a friend *and* a sexual object. This works best in situations where the woman can see Jackson around a lot, hopefully in informal settings. That way, Jackson doesn't have to push the sexual envelope too fast and risk a rejection before the woman knows what she is rejecting.

In this case, The Smooth had a very good chance of success, because Sirenna had the chance to furtively check out his body over time and observe how he carried himself in a flock of women.

I was getting impatient. Allen was being a prick again, in his own conniving way. He gave me a project that involved a client presentation in dreaded Sioux Falls, South Dakota, even though the client was a friend and would have met me in Chicago.

I asked Allen to let me do the gig in Chicago, but he insisted I go to Sioux Falls. WTF? Had he heard me carrying on in the break room about how much I hated staying in Sioux Falls? Our corporate hotel there was the pits—I was even bitten by bedbugs once.

After the promotion incident, Allen continued to make dismissive comments about my qualifications. He had the nerve to tell me to finish my MBA. In the big picture, he was not wrong. But I felt he minimized my on-the-job performance.

Somehow, he could see right through me with his needle-y eyes. I felt like Allen could see what a depraved slut I was, hidden so expertly in my corporate persona. I didn't usually feel so naked around a colleague. I felt naked around Jackson in my power suit—an incredibly hot feeling. With most of my male co-workers, I felt totally in control, able to reel them in whenever I wanted. But Allen was unaffected by my demanding hips. I could just feel him passing judgment. *Yuck!*

"C'mon, Jackson!" I said impatiently, after the third week in aerobics class had yielded nothing ... unless you consider a five minute chat with Sirenna at the water cooler a breakthrough.

"I got this!" Jackson assured me over spiked tea. "I got this!"

What Jackson didn't tell me was that Sirenna had been looking him over more thoroughly while they talked. Women are very careful about staring, but Sirenna was starting to gaze. Jackson tells me that when a girl stops being discreet and brazenly stares, that means she is getting more comfortable with him. It also means she is advancing the intention within herself. The primal attraction is taking hold, whether she is conscious of it or not.

Then, he tells me, it's simply a matter of maintaining a comfortable vibe, getting the woman into an environment where one thing can lead to another.

Given that this was a more delicate situation involving a married woman who hadn't crossed the line before, that environment would usually include alcohol.

It wasn't until the fourth week of aerobics classes that Jackson came home, gave me a hug, and said with that wicked smile of his, "It's time."

The final phase of the plot was now in play—get Chelsea off to her friends for the night, choose outfits, and practice our back stories.

That Friday morning, Jackson headed off to work.

I gave him a bigger hug than usual, then grabbed his crotch. "Make sure that monster is ready. I'm counting on you," I told him. He just laughed.

This time, I went to the aerobics class. Jackson did not.

When Sirenna saw me, she came up and gave me a big hug. "Great to see you!" she said. "We've missed you in the group."

Awkward silence. I didn't really exit the group with grace. It was more like I slinked out.

"What are you doing here?"

"Well, my Stairmaster broke," I said, which was technically true. "This class was recommended to me."

"Well, the instructor's not bad," Sirenna said, "but some of the students are ...." I saw her looking past the glass doors, but no Jackson—if that's who she was searching for.

A flash of disappointment perhaps? But then she grabbed me and pulled me over to where she was stretching. "What are you doing after? You want to get a drink?"

"I've been trying to cut down," I said. Again, technically true, though in a halfhearted way. Then I whispered, "But with both our marriages on the rocks, we could do worse than a couple of shots."

Sirenna's laugh trailed into something else, and a plan was set.

Four hours later, we were in a loud bar, in the throes of happy hour.

Sirenna and I got along like sorority sisters. It was a classic girls' night out, swapping off-color stories while being interrupted by annoying guys from time to time, both of us enjoying the attention that two girls on their game can get.

We took a "men can go fuck themselves!" shot followed by a sloppy playful kiss. I lingered on the kiss a bit longer than I intended. Sirenna didn't seem to mind, and I was struck by her angular beauty. She was right off of a 1970s movie set—full-figured, loaded with sex and longing.

I excused myself to go to the ladies' room, leaving her to fend for herself with two adorably nerdy tech dudes who had plucked up the nerve to chat us up. What they were doing in a sports bar, I had no idea. I wanted to ask them, but the game was afoot.

I locked myself in a stall and texted Jackson. *We're at the Red Zone. Come soon.*

Thirty minutes later, still in the midst of a loud conversation with our sexually aspiring computer dudes, Jackson showed up looking hulky and casual. Sirenna, well plied with alcohol, ran and gave him a big ol' hug, as if they were old friends. *Grrr* ....

"Jackson! What are you doing here?"

"Meeting my basketball team," Jackson said, glancing at his phone. "But I just realized I'm early."

"Well, you can kill the time with us!" yelled Sirenna, her eyes lighting up as if a director had called "action." The nerdy dudes, Jeff and Matthias, seemed pretty bummed out by Jackson's presence. He had a way of frustrating guys who like to woo women with witty remarks.

"Do you know Jackson?" Sirenna said, almost possessively.

"Yeah," I said, glad she couldn't see the pictures of Jackson and me frolicking on my phone.

"We were on the same softball team a couple years ago," Jackson offered helpfully. The line came off as a bit forced, but Sirenna didn't really notice. She took Jackson under her wing to get him a drink, as if I wasn't there. Double *grrr* ....

I entertained myself with the nerdy dudes. They meant well enough, but I've never understood why some guys play the wrong game. Matthias and Jeff would have made lovely boyfriends, but they were out of their element here. And the girls hanging out weren't husband shopping. The guys were telling me how they once stole their final exam out from under their professor's nose, acing their last college class—despite missing a ton of lectures. It wasn't the most believable story.

Then Jeff launched right into the next anecdote, something about solving a formula on the whiteboard like Matt Damon in *Good Will Hunting*. But there were no Matt Damons here.

"Excuse me." I grabbed his hand. I could not afford to let this evening slip. "What's your friend's name again?"

"Matthias," he said.

"Look, Jeff and Matthias," I said, pulling them close as if for physical support, or to tell them a secret. I had downed a couple drinks myself, and had been prone to speaking freely of late.

"You see that big guy over there?" I told them. "Well, his name is Jackson. Tonight he is going to fuck me and Sirenna with his huge cock until we both pass out."

The looks on Jeff's and Matthias' faces were priceless. No more blustering, witty anecdotes. Just delicious, pregnant silence. Jeff seemed a bit hurt, which gave me a flash of guilt as Brad and Daniel popped into my head. *Ugh!*

One more jealous look at Jackson and they were off, leaving me feeling bad for overdoing it. I had used a hammer when a polite comment would have been enough. *God, I am a bitch!* But I couldn't let that distract me now ....

I pulled my chair noisily between the two of them, turning Jackson, Sirenna, and me into a threesome.

"Awww, what did you say, Corrie?" Sirenna asked. "I thought those guys were cute."

"Not my type," I said. "I need a little more meat on the bone."

Sirenna flushed and Jackson laughed, perhaps enjoying our little pretense.

Then, in accordance with our machinations, Jackson excused himself to "call his boys." "Too loud in here," he said, making his way outside.

That left Sirenna and me huddled against the bar, giggling like schoolgirls.

"I think he likes you," I said, ribbing her with my elbow.

"You think?" Sirenna said. "God, he is such a .... If I were ever going to cheat on my husband, that's the guy I'd do it with."

"No arguments here!" I said.

Sirenna laughed, but too innocently.

I had not gotten the point across. *Let's try this*: "I've fucked Jackson before."

Silence ... savoring the shock value. Then Sirenna blurted out, "*Whaaaat*? You never said you cheated on your husband."

Hmm .... I had to think hard about what to say next. "When your husband cheats on you, all bets are off," I said. "I just ... wasn't ready to tell the group. My own desires just seemed so ...."

More silence. Sirenna gave me a couple hard looks, perhaps jealous, perhaps judgmental. But curious.

"And …."

"And what?"

"And how *was* he?" she finally blurted out.

Nice dripping silence ….

Then I looked her square in the face. "Best goddamn fuck of my life."

Sirenna sucked her drink down. "Really?"

"Oh yes," I told her, "and it's not even close."

"Details!" she demanded, pulling me close.

"He's just … born to fuck," I said, letting my mind wander lustfully, relieved to be done with the lying.

Even in this cavern of noise, I had Sirenna's complete attention, her eyes movie star wide.

"He can last forever, for one thing," I said.

Sirenna seemed to be taking on water, like a slowly leaking boat.

"And he just knows, you know, how to touch you and when. The boy's got rhythm, that's all." I shrugged.

Sirenna wanted more. "And …?"

I wasn't giving it up easily. She would have to work for it.

"And …"? I repeated, raising an eyebrow.

More silence, but then, "What about his cock?"

"What about it?"

"Is it … well …."

"Yeah, it's fucking big." I finally gave her what she wanted to hear.

A look of satisfaction flashed across her face. And, if I wasn't wrong, determination.

"It's fucking perfect," I added.

"But it's cheating …" Sirenna said, though I'm not sure if she meant that as a rebuke to me or to her own reeling mind.

"Girl, when a man fucks you that good, it's cheating yourself *not* to do it."

Sirenna looked at me long and hard, as if pondering a deep riddle.

"I've got problems in my marriage, all right, but I've *never* regretted fucking Jackson," I told her. It was the closest thing to a lie I said to her that night. But also the closest thing to the truth.

Sirenna looked confused, but also … deep in thought. Perhaps deep in forbidden thoughts.

"Well, my husband *is* out of town," Sirenna said wistfully. "He's not due back till tomorrow."

"Look," I said, "I can't tell you how to fix your marriage—God knows I can't fix mine. All I can tell you is that you need to get seriously laid. It will help you figure out the rest."

"Are you sure?" Sirenna asked doubtfully. "I'm not sure if I'm ready to be alone with him. I don't know him that well."

"Oh, I can help you there," I said. "Just invite both of us back to your house for a nightcap. From there, we can make sure it's a good vibe; then I can head out. Or, if you'd like, I can keep an eye out while you scream."

Sirenna looked surprised and embarrassed. But she cracked a smile, knowing I meant screams of pleasure, not terror.

Jackson was on his way back. We were about to find out.

Chapter 19

"SEIZE YOUR CHANCE," I hissed in Sirenna's ear. We got back to drinking and chit-chat, but Sirenna didn't seem as happy and relaxed. She seemed nervous, closed up. I started to think our plan was on the rocks.

Then she said, "Hey, you two. I wanna kick my shoes off and have a drink at home. You guys want to join me?"

Jackson was up for it. I grabbed my purse.

Jackson went with Sirenna in her car; I followed behind. I felt my first big thigh-tingle just thinking of the two of them together talking nervously, but sensing the erotic tug between them. I worked my stick-shift with some extra push.

Her house wasn't in the mansion part of town like I'd expected. It was just a modest, normal, two-story place with a bench swing on the front porch. Anywhere America … and I don't mean that in a bad way.

Sirenna let us in. Jackson and I exchanged a furtive glance and followed. We had not really discussed what would happen if he, or we, actually got Sirenna alone. Maybe that was why things went bad. I dunno.

Awkwardness kicked in. That's the problem with drinking

versus marijuana—if you've had a few drinks and suddenly go to a stranger's house, it can still feel weird. Pot can smooth that out, but Sirenna wasn't the type.

Maybe the tiny Grandma kitchen table wasn't the best place to loosen up either. Jackson and I sat there while Sirenna made the rum and Cokes. We ended up hunkering over the table like we were at a stale frat party that was winding down. Yet it was still early, only 8 p.m.

Then I had an inspiration. "Oh no!"

"What?" the two of them said.

"I forgot my Fitbit at the club. I took it off to show those guys my workout times."

It was a small lie. I had taken the darned thing off in the car because it was itching my hand. My daughter got it for me and I was forcing myself to wear it, but I needed to do something about the fit.

Before they could protest, I was on the phone calling the club and out the front door, waving a casual goodbye. I didn't have time to coordinate with Jackson, and I didn't dare text him. But he knew what to do. I just hoped Sirenna would feel safe enough ….

No trip to the club for me. Just a nice drive down the expressway, radio surfing. "Free Fallin' " by Tom Petty, then Katy Perry, then the Black Eyed Peas. The last two made me smile. Fergie of the Black Eyed Peas recently confessed her love of well-endowed men, and Katy Perry is also a size queen—or so the tabloids say, not to mention her song lyrics. Doing bad things was on my mind.

Sirenna's front door was shut when I pulled in. I made a point of switching the lock so it would open behind me. Sure enough, it opened.

No sign of Sirenna or Jackson. The kitchen table still had drinks on it.

Maybe the living room? No. Dark.

The back patio? No.

Where, then?

I tried the door behind the kitchen—nothing, except creepy cellar steps. Wrong movie! Then, off the living room, I found a short set of stairs I had missed. Was that a shirt on the floor? I fumbled for a light switch.

Why yes, it was. And that was *definitely* a bra.

It seemed a fair bet his trail of clothes would lead me to my husband and his conquest. I thought I could hear a noise, and then, around the corner, yes, a slurping sound.

Through a wide-open bedroom door, a buck-naked Sirenna was kneeling on the ground before Jackson, her hands on his sides, trying to get his cock into her mouth.

She looked so sexy, her big breasts swinging, her panties flung to one side of the room and dangling on the handle of a Stairmaster. *That horny bitch must have literally ripped her clothes off*, I thought.

Sirenna took a break from licking and massaging his penis to stare at it adoringly. "It's … so big," I heard her say.

But then she must have noticed my movement, because she whipped her head around and belted out a blood-curdling scream.

Sirenna must have thought it was her husband. This was going south, and fast.

"It's okay, Sirenna, chill," I whispered, a bit squeamish at the prospect of her neighbors calling 911.

"Corrie, what the …?"

I shut the bedroom door, but that had the wrong effect. Sirenna got a crazy look in her eyes, as if some horrible scene from *True Crime* was unfolding. Maybe it was her fear of getting caught by her prick of a husband, but she looked like she could crawl the wall at any moment.

For the first time in my short history of corrupting other men's wives, I felt seriously shitty. Sirenna's terrified look is one I will never be able to erase from my memory completely.

I had to calm her down, and quick. Even Jackson looked

uncertain. So I said the one unfathomable thing that might cut through the crazy in her head.

"Sirenna, Jackson is my husband."

Silence. Disbelief. But her body stopped shaking and she put the bra she had grabbed back down.

"Yes. Jackson and I have been married for twelve years. He's here … because of me."

"What?!"

Sirenna's fright had given way to disbelief, which was, under the circumstances, preferable. She slowly sat down on the bed.

I sat down next to her. "Jackson and I … We're having issues in our marriage."

"And this is … your idea of how you fix it?" Sirenna was incredulous.

"Well, since you put it that way … yes," I said. "How do I put this …." I spoke slowly, as if I were a guest on *Jerry Springer*. Except there had never been a Springer episode like this one.

I suddenly realized how I could play this. "In the last few years, I've come to realize that Jackson, well, he has a rare ability—a gift, I guess you could say."

"A gift? You mean—"

"Well, yes, he does have a wonderful penis, but it's not just that." I continued, "He's just so much better at pleasing women, Sirenna. He knows how badly we need it … and how to take it from us."

"Take it from us?" she repeated.

I thought I saw the first signs of lust on her face. But she went back on the attack. "If what you say is true—if he's everything you say he is—then why don't you just keep him to yourself?"

I wasn't giving away *all* my secrets. Besides, she knew Jackson had cheated on me. "Well, I realized, for one thing, I enjoy watching Jackson take other men's wives."

"Enough to get yourself in some serious trouble!" Sirenna said indignantly.

"Yes," I sighed. Oh what the hell, why not go for it: "And I like to see him give frustrated wives something they have *never* felt before," I asserted.

I thought I saw Sirenna's cheeks flush.

"And," I went on, trying to decide if this wasn't too absurd, "and I think that keeping Jackson to myself, well, it's selfish. It's like asking a world-class violinist not to play in an orchestra."

"Well that is *the* most ridiculous thing I have heard a woman say, in, maybe … ever!" Sirenna stammered.

But that was my opening. "Oh yeah?" I said, rising to the challenge. "Well, if you think it's so ridiculous, then why don't we find out?" I motioned Jackson to stand. He followed my lead, towering above her. She looked uncertain, but his penis was staring back at her, swaying a little, soft but still obscenely real.

"I don't think this is a good idea at all!" Sirenna protested, but Jackson and I knew he had won. I gave him a forceful nod.

He put her right hand directly on his penis. "That's it, Sirenna, stroke it. You know you want to," he insisted.

Sirenna gave another look of protest, but she didn't pull her hand away. She kept it firm around his cock, marveling at its fullness.

"It's so … warm, so thick," she said, gazing up at it, and then at him.

I pressed against the closet door, removing myself from her line of vision.

Then Jackson did the one thing that could still surprise me. It probably surprised Sirenna too. He knelt down and kissed her soulfully, enough to make that sweet/scary jealousy shoot up my spine.

That did the trick. Sirenna dropped his penis and started making out with him, like a teenager on her third date. She ran her hands down his rippling back as they kneeled together. Her beautiful breasts mashed up against him while they made out.

This make-out session went on for a long time, with her not

even acknowledging his penis. Something about the innocence of it was *so* hot. I leaned against the closet wall in the shadows, working my hand down to my pussy, which was about to go from wet to sopping.

If you didn't know better, you'd think this was just two kids skipping band practice to make out behind the bleachers. But Sirenna's gobsmackingly mature breasts were one clue that this might be more than two youngsters. The other was Jackson's big thick penis, as hard as I'd *ever* seen it, pushed up between then, nudging ominously against her belly.

But she didn't reach down for it—not yet. The only clue this encounter might have the potential to go past first base was the swaying of her hips as she kissed him in long stretches, mumbling, "Oh, Jackson …" to catch her breath.

He had melted this girl's terror to fresh clay for his pottery wheel. Was he going to make love to her, tenderly, as if taking her virginity for the first time?

Then, without a pause in the kissing, Sirenna slid her hand down to his cock, stroking it. I was envious, thinking about the first time I made out with Jackson while holding his huge cock, feeling my pussy warm like an oven on preheat.

So much for innocence. Sirenna started rubbing Jackson's big dick up and down her pussy as she held on to his neck. Even in the shadowy lamp light, I could see the sheen of his cock bathed with her juices. Between kisses, her mewls started turning into moans. I felt the urge to rub myself grow myself stronger, along with my desire to see Jackson conquer this woman, forever inserting a wedge between her and her dick of a husband.

Then, as if he could read my diabolical thoughts, Jackson lifted Sirenna up and pushed her down on the bed—hard. "This is what you came for, not a make-out session!" Jackson scolded, slapping his cock down on Sirenna's stomach as she gasped. I expected her to ask for my permission or help, but she surprised me, kicking her legs up in the air instead.

"Oh god, yes! Please fuck me, Jackson!"

I waited for Jackson to work his cock into Sirenna gradually, giving her time to warm up as he always did with a new conquest. But he must have known something—in that Jackson "slut whisperer" way—because he shoved it in with one hard stroke and easily put the entire thing into her pussy.

"Oh wow, Jackson!"

Jeez, I thought, *Allen must have a bigger dick than I thought. Or else her pussy is big.*

Sensing his advantage, Jackson immediately pinned Sirenna's wrists down and started thrusting.

Two strokes in and, "Cumming …!"

She thrust her hips up while he held her ass. It wasn't a big cum, but still …. If she came that hard after a few strokes, what would happen next?

I thought Allen was going to lay into her, but instead he pulled out with a massive wet plop and flipped Sirenna over. And boy was I glad he did! On Sirenna's back was a massive black tattoo, a serpent that went from the crack of her ass all the way up to the flames on her neck.

Now THAT was a side of Sirenna I wasn't expecting. Jackson *loves* tattooed girls; he has this notion they are more sexual and more aggressive about seeking out big cocks. He smiled his approval. As Jackson jammed his cock up into her, I realized what he was doing. Seeing how Sirenna had accommodated him with ease, he proceeded to one of the toughest positions to take a big cock if you're new to it.

"Oh god!" Sirenna said. Jackson wasn't thrusting hard yet, but he was already balls deep inside her. Sirenna moved her ass around on his cock, and she was twitching and cumming again. "Fuck, that dick feels amazing," Sirenna said.

"Oh girl, you don't know the half of it!" I told her, knowing full well that Jackson was still just toying with her.

I was on the verge of moving out of the shadows for a closer look. For some reason, I held onto the closet door instead.

It's a good thing I did. Before anyone had time to think, a man barged into the room and started punching Jackson in the back.

Chapter 20

"**S**IRENNA, YOU BITCH!" HE yelled. *Allen. Yes, my boss … Allen. Allen!!!*

Allen looked enraged, and he was the kind of guy who would keep a gun in his room.

Fuck, this was *not* good!

I surged into husband-in-danger mode, grabbing a laundry bag from behind me that had some dirties in it and throwing it over Allen's head from behind. I don't think he even saw me. The bag disoriented him enough for me to push him down into a desk chair.

As Jackson held his arms down, I kept the bag over his head. I could *not* let Allen see me.

Sirenna hopped up.

"Sirenna, what the fuck is going on?!" Allen said, enraged. His voice was muffled; I worried he might be struggling to breathe.

I expected Sirenna to rush to Allen's defense. After all, two near-strangers were holding her husband down. But the tattoo was not the only surprising thing about her.

"What do you think, Allen? I was fucking around on

you! Just like you did on me," Sirenna said indignantly. The situation was hardly comical; still, I tried not to laugh at the sight of a buck-naked woman yelling angrily at her husband, who couldn't see a damn thing anyhow.

"Sirenna, you let me go immediately!" Allen said. I have to give him credit. He sounded more angry than scared.

Allen tried to double up his arms and break Jackson's hold, but Jackson wasn't letting go. Allen flailed.

"Everyone in this room who is *not* my wife is going to jail," Allen threatened. But I was still confused by Sirenna's behavior. Why wasn't she rushing to his defense?

"Hold him here, Corrie. I'll be right back."

Ugh! Sirenna left the room, but the damage was done.

"Corrie?" Allen let that sink in. We all did. No choice. The silence was brutal. Then the inevitable, "Corrie from work?"

Oh shit. Sirenna!

I didn't say anything. But my silence said plenty. Jackson and I exchanged a glance. *WTF?*

Allen fell into silence. The shock of his wife somehow conspiring with his subordinate seemed to have stunned him.

Sirenna came back in into the room, carrying a big roll of duct tape.

Allen found his voice. "Corrie, you are *so fired*. You are done. Whatever you are doing here, you are … *fucked*!!"

Sirenna kneeled down behind the chair, signaling to Jackson to help tape his hands.

"No, honey," Sirenna said in a calm, steely voice, "it's you who are fucked. Or more accurately, it's me who was getting fucked, and I'm not done yet."

Allen was having none of it. "Help!" he screamed. "Heeeeeelp!!"

This wasn't okay. Allen had to be stopped. Fuck it; he knew who I was anyhow.

I pulled the bag off his head and put my hand over his mouth.

Allen spit on my hand, trying to scream through it. I was

terrified he would bite me. Jackson looked like he was about to punch Allen in the face. That wasn't good. So, without thinking, I punched Allen in the eye. And just like that, he was out. *Whoops*.

Secretly, I was kind of proud of myself. I had reflexively used one of my self-defense punches. But maybe now hadn't been the right time.

"Oh shit! I'm sorry, Sirenna …. Is he okay?"

"He'd better be!" she said. For the first time, I could see concern for her husband. I could see that wild, uncertain look in her eyes returning. *Ugh*.

Jackson went to work checking his pulse. "He's still breathing," he said. "He's just … knocked out."

"Should we call someone?" I asked. I was afraid of law enforcement, but even more afraid of what might happen if ….

"No," said Sirenna. "Not yet. Let's just wait and see if he comes around."

So, in the most surreal moment in my sexual history, that's what we did. The three of us sat next to one another at the end of the bed, staring at Sirenna's husband, hands tied, head down. Sirenna put a robe on. Jackson had slipped on some boxer shorts.

We sat in silence, staring intently at Allen, pondering our fates.

"What the fuck just happened?" I finally blurted out. We almost broke out laughing, but not quite.

"And what the fuck are you two up to?" Sirenna asked. "Wait …." *Oh shit!* She must be flashing back to meeting Jackson in class, then "randomly" meeting the two of us in a bar down the line. And then the connect with her and me from the support group. She was putting the pieces together in her mind. *No!*

Things might have gotten *much* worse, but her thought process was interrupted when Allen jerked his head up, glaring at us. With his black eye and ruffled hair, hands taped back, he looked more comical than threatening—except for the small matter that he was my boss. I could vaguely feel my knuckles throbbing now.

"Oh, honey …" Sirenna said. I couldn't tell if it was genuine concern or mockery. "Are you okay?" She was looking at his eye and ruffling his hair.

Allen wasn't humoring her with a straight answer. "You're in serious fucking trouble," he snarled.

I signaled to Jackson that we should leave, and he grabbed his pants.

"Oh no … *you're* not going anywhere!" Sirenna said to both of us, but specifically to Jackson.

Then Sirenna did something I'll never forget: with one swift move, she ripped a piece of tape off the roll and applied it to Allen's mouth. Then another, to seal it down. This one she wrapped around the back of his head.

Allen immediately starting bucking and protesting, but now it was just a muffled yelp.

"Don't buck like that, Allen!" Sirenna chided him. "Stay calm and breathe through your nose." She kneeled in front of him and looked him right in the eye. "I was in the middle of getting *fucked*, and I'm not stopping until it's done! You've fucked around on me, and now it's time for payback. And you're gonna watch!"

With that last line, I could see Allen's body shift. It was almost as if the chance to watch his gorgeous wife was too alluring to resist, even in this state.

And with that, Sirenna seductively pulled her robe aside and pushed Jackson onto the bed.

With his boxers still on, she worked Jackson's cock out of his fly. Jackson wasn't hard yet; his criminal activities must have messed with this boner. But it was always hot to watch a girl work Jackson's cock to erection. Even now it was flopping into shape in her hands, improbably growing and thickening.

This time, for some strange reason, I remembered condoms.

And from the way Sirenna was working her ass up in the air, we were going to need them fast.

"Condoms!" I said.

Sirenna looked up from licking Jackson's cock and pointed to a drawer next to her bed.

I got the condoms out, then laughed as I picked up the wrapper.

"*Slim* fit? This will never work on Jackson!"

"Oh yeah, I forgot!" Sirenna said, now working Jackson's spit-drenched cock with two hands.

I couldn't help laughing. *Fuck it;* my job was already lost. After all the grief Allen had given me, the look of shame on his face was gratifying.

"Let's try this anyway!" Sirenna said, working to put Allen's condom on Jackson's penis. Corrie, can you help so it won't break?"

I kneeled on the other side of my husband and helped Sirenna move the top of Allen's condom over Jackson's head.

But it wasn't going to work. We couldn't even stretch the condom across Jackson's wide head. After one more pull, it broke.

More laughter.

"That's it … I'm not waiting any longer!" Sirenna said, daring me to tell her to stop.

I did. "Wait …" I said, digging in my purse. I always kept a few Durex XXL condoms handy now; they had proven more reliable than the Magnums. Sirenna took it from me reluctantly. She'd clearly hoped for a bareback ride, but that wasn't happening. She put the condom on with urgency, and this one fit over most of Jackson's cock. It was still tight.

"Oh, that's nice and snug," Sirenna said, obviously turned on by Jackson's shiny cock wrapped in plastic, ready to please her pussy.

Without waiting any longer, she mounted Jackson, her back to Allen. She was cramping up, trying to squat over him.

"Dammit!" I heard her say, but after some trial and error, she straddled him with her long legs, positioning herself above his penis. Then she slid down onto it, and most of his cock plunged inside her with a *squelch*.

"Oh …" I heard her say, working it up and down. She reached behind him, checking to see if there was more dick outside of her. There was. "I want it all in!" she said.

Jackson adjusted his hips and pulled her down as he thrust up. I heard a popping sound and then he was balls deep.

"Ohhhhhh," Sirenna said. "I have never …."

If she was shy about fucking a married man in front of her husband, that shyness was drowning in lust. Soon she was thrusting up and down, her back starting to glisten from the intensity of her thrusts. I was mesmerized by the serpent sliding up and down as she moved. Allen seemed to be also; he was in a daze.

I felt a twinge of jealousy as Sirenna took Jackson deeper and faster than I ever had. If I did it that fast, sometimes it was too much. Sirenna appeared to have no such problem—slut!—and I knew that deep, fast rhythm was going to make her come hard.

But I had no idea how hard. Maybe she didn't either.

"I'm cumming again …" Sirenna said. But it wasn't just a cum—it was her body undergoing tremors, shaking from head to toes. She had to brace herself on Jackson's chest, planting her pussy hard on Jackson to keep him inside.

"Oh my god!" Sirenna cooed.

"There's more cum inside you," Jackson assured her, staying firmly planted.

"I don't know if I can …" Sirenna mewled. But Jackson showed her how. Instead of thrusting up and down, he held her down with his big penis deep inside her, and showed her how to rotate in wide circles, bending with his big penis but never losing him.

"Oh …" Sirenna said.

More jealousy from me … but it didn't stop me from touching myself. I leaned against the closet so it would be harder for Allen to see me, but at this point I didn't care enough to sweat it further. Like Sirenna, I needed my orgasm.

As Jackson moved Sirenna's hips in big circles around his cock, the woman was in a trance. "Oh wow, Jackson, I have *never* fucked like this before."

I knew what she meant. You can do this position with smaller cocks, but not in those big wide circles. And there's something about that circular rhythm. Slow and steady, slow and steady ….

"Now … you're gonna cum," said Jackson.

And it happened. It was almost a growl like you hear building up inside a female lion on a nature show … and it grew and grew until her hips and ass just started shaking and quaking—even though she was barely thrusting. It was just too much.

"Oh my fucking god! Oh my god!! Oh, my Gawwwwwwd!"

I knew that kind of cum. It was the monster orgasm that wipes the slate clean.

I was glad to see Sirenna didn't squirt—that was one thing I didn't want her to have over me, given that she could handle Jackson's penis so well. I hadn't managed to squirt after that first time and had given up trying. I can only imagine what it felt like for him to see this beautiful woman screaming and trembling in years of pent-up gratitude, head lying down on his chest for support.

My own legs clenched together. My fingers had done their magic and I was spasming as well.

Oh ….

That was the best finger/clit self-orgasm I'd had in the longest time, and I didn't even realize I was doing it until I blew.

Sirenna pulled Jackson's cock out of her, but before it came all the way out, she reached back and held the condom on.

I guess that meant she wasn't done.

Turns out Jackson wasn't done either. He pushed her back

into doggy style and took her as savagely as I'd *ever* seen a woman be taken. Sirenna was coming continuously, screaming and wailing and yelling in tongues. Jackson had her hair in one hand, pulling her back while slapping her ass so hard you could see the redness.

"You love this cock, bitch!" Jackson taunted.

"Oh god, yes! Fuck you, Jackson! Fuck you!"

I laughed. I'd heard that before. Some women need to get angry with Jackson when they cum.

But as he slammed harder, she started working her ass back up in the air, almost a foot at a time, while he pounded back. It was a frenzy of thrashing fucking, like the peak of a Metallica song or something.

"Fuck me, Jackson! Fuck me with your big black dick!! Oh … my …."

Oh, boy. She was really losing it. And just like that, Sirenna gripped the sheets with both hands as if an earthquake was coming—it was—and Jackson kept his cock inside her, clutching her thighs to hold her in place. Sirenna was convulsing, unable to speak, flopping and convulsing in a new world of ecstasy and sensation. She was being owned.

With that, Jackson pulled out, but he took care to hold the condom on, sensing Sirenna wasn't done. No, she wasn't. But the last cum had been cathartic for her. She was now back in reality—enough, I think, to remember that her husband was tied up, watching the show. I couldn't get a read on Allen, but I could tell he wasn't missing a second of this.

With one swift move, Sirenna turned around and straddled Jackson so she could face her husband directly. She worked Jackson's penis inside her with a groan, thrusting up and down at a leisurely pace, as if she fucked big eight-inch cocks all the time.

That's when she started to lose it with her husband.

"Allen, see this? See this?! This is what I needed, Allen. You had no right to cheat on me. I was the one who needed another dick. And oh, do I know that now!" She started riding Jackson a bit faster. "Oh god, do I know!"

For the first time since she took on Jackson, Allen started to moan—a muffled moan through the tape, but a moan nonetheless.

That's when she called out to me.

"Corrie, please help Allen. I'm sure he wants to cum and you've tied his hands up."

I didn't know what to say. Allen looked over at me with a hostile, depraved look, but the hostility faded into something sicker and sweeter.

Whatever was done, was done. It wasn't like I was getting my job back. And a part of me was curious—curious to see the cock of a man who was so confident and powerful at work.

So I buttoned up my jeans—no free looks for Allen—and kneeled behind him. I reached both hands around the chair and managed to find my way to Allen's fly. I could feel something hard in there. I unzipped it while Corrie thrust lightly up and down, watching us intensely.

After a bit of fussing with Allen's fly, out popped the hardest—and tiniest—penis I had ever seen. It couldn't have been much more than four inches, probably less. But it was really thin too. Thin as a tampon.

"See, Corrie? See what I've been trying to work with?"

I could see what Sirenna wanted from me, but I wasn't ready to humiliate Allen. I was still too worried about his retribution. However, I did stroke him, marveling at how I could handle him with just two fingers.

That was good enough for Sirenna. She seemed extra turned on now, thrusting while staring intently at my hand stroking Allen's dick.

"Stroke that tiny penis, Corrie. See how fast he cums!"

I was still amazed at the feeling of stroking Allen; it was like stroking a large magic marker. *How could he and Jackson even be the same gender?*

I felt a wave of compassion for angry, fucked-up Allen. It must be really difficult to strut around, knowing women are attracted to your power, but knowing you can't possibly please their pussies with your dick, no matter how much office space you acquire. No wonder he was trapped in his fucked-up psychology.

I started jacking Allen with my entire hand, completely hiding his cock.

Allen was bucking in my hand, and I could tell he wasn't going to last long. I suddenly had this image of Allen letting go and squirting in my face, which is exactly what he did—one quick but intense burst, rocketing from his tiny penis directly into my face. A couple more drips that missed, but the damage was done.

Even Jackson laughed.

"Ugh!" was all I could say, staggering toward the distant bathroom light to get Allen's yuck off of me.

Sirenna was too far into her own ecstasy now to worry about my mess. Riding Jackson this way, she couldn't bounce up and down as hard, so she settled on a slower, sensual rhythm. Jackson thrust slowly up as she pushed out, keeping his cock inside her.

By then, I had the cum off me and returned, standing behind Allen as if I was his keeper. It was beautiful to watch Jackson's penis moving in and out, pulling Sirenna's pussy lips along with it. So much friction! That was a wonderful sensation, having your lips tugged from such a thick cock. It must feel incredible to her, given Allen was way too tiny to possibly pull her lips inside out.

Lucky girl …. Dammit, Sirenna!

To distract myself, I returned to Allen, whose sticky little penis throbbed and perked to life when I touched it. Sirenna wasn't going to last long. Those slow, full strokes were getting to her, making her legs tremble and shake. Then she sat down on Jackson and stopped moving.

This had the effect of pushing his cock into her and holding it in place, absorbing her spasms. But it also braced Sirenna so she wouldn't fall off the bed, which she might have done otherwise. Her eyes were rolling. For a minute, I thought she might drool fluid from her mouth like the girl from *The Exorcist*. No more screams from Sirenna, just a massive erotic silence as her body exhaled.

And that was too much for Allen as well. Before he could even get fully hard again, his tiny penis squirted. This time I held my hand up but there was no need—only a few drops were left as Allen's hips bucked helplessly. I felt Allen gripping the chair and thrusting into my hand.

Sirenna seemed like she had been adequately conquered. She lifted herself off Jackson, and her pussy made a series of unflattering exhales. That's the downside of having a cock like Jackson's expelled from your pussy—not so ladylike.

Sirenna laughed, and her face reddened. "Your cock … it's a revelation," she said to Jackson.

Then came the strangest experience I've ever had with another couple. Instead of finishing the scene, instead of chit-chat, I just locked eyes with Jackson and nodded toward the door. He dressed quickly and silently, not even taking the condom off. I zipped up my jeans and adjusted my blouse. My pussy was sopping wet, but that would have to wait. We needed to get out of here.

Sirenna, meanwhile, was splayed on the bed. She seemed like she was barely conscious, or if she was, she didn't care to say a word.

Allen, meanwhile, had the look of a puppy that had escaped into the yard and run until it was exhausted. He was so defeated, he didn't even seem to care that his mouth was still covered in tape.

But I knew Allen would regain his glare soon. For a brief moment, I wondered how I would ever face him at work. I wouldn't just lose my job; I wouldn't have much of a career left if he had anything to say about it.

We left the room without saying a word, Sirenna laid out and Allen slumped in his chair, his arms still restrained. Add a bit of blood on Sirenna's body and it would have been a police scene.

"Fuck, what the hell was that?" I said to Jackson as he opened the car door for me, the gentleman of strange circumstances.

Jackson showed a hint of a smile, but I could tell he was shaken as well.

A few blocks away, I told Jackson to pull over. I unzipped his pants, pulled the condom off his penis and tossed it into a gutter. Not very eco-nice, but I didn't want that girl's juices on him.

"This is the last time we are *ever* doing anything like this!" I told him.

He nodded. At the time, I meant it. I suddenly felt very vanilla. It was as if all the kink, all the deviation had been purged out of my body. We hadn't done any violence to Allen, but we had done violence to his marriage. They say serial killers want to go from one kill to a bigger and more intense one. But not me. I never wanted to kill like this again.

Speaking of problems, Jackson and I had one on the home front that night. We were both in dire need of sleep, but both of us were too worked up.

"Dammit," he said, once we were in bed.

"What, honey?" I said, my arms around him.

"My balls ...."

Jackson had told me about blue balls before. I'd given him a big case of them the night we met. I was always fascinated and skeptical about this peculiar male hang-up—it seemed like an excuse to push a girl's sexual envelope and whine.

He assured me that blue balls were real, and I always humored him. "I don't want to fuck, but I'll make you cum," I said.

And with that, I jacked him off, patiently and almost clinically. On most days he would have needed a more determined approach, but he had been inside Sirenna's pussy, getting all warmed up, so it was simply a matter of increasing my rhythm, two hands moving up and down his big sticky penis. I slapped a condom on him before he could blow, which comes in handy when your husband spurts a ton of fluid you don't need on your sheets. Rope after rope filled the tip of the condom. How he cums so much more than a small guy like Allen I'll never know, but the sight makes me really fucking wet. For a moment I wished that spray had gone against my walls. Another time.

With a happy grunt, Jackson's business was done. I had a big cum in me too, but I was too preoccupied with the collapse of my professional career to think about that. Unlike Jackson, I don't get blue balls, exactly. I just get a dull ache that actually pays off if I can let it build for a day or two. Right now, I wasn't feeling it. I fell asleep with my hand casually holding Jackson's floppy penis.

"This monster has gotten us into a shitload of trouble, baby," I said to him. He laughed, which ticked me off. I had a serious point to make, but I fell asleep before I could connect the thoughts.

Chapter 21

I WOKE UP EARLY, with a vague memory of Jackson leaning down in his new overalls and kissing me. I was still in a daze. I surprised myself by sleeping pretty soundly. I guess when you throw your future away, there isn't much to do but sleep it off.

I must have looked like I would never leave the bed again. Jackson asked if he should stay home with me. I told him no—I wasn't staying in bed either. Quick kiss, Jackson revved his truck.

A few glorious snooze alarms later, I dragged my ass out of bed. Time to face this professional Waterloo. *Ugh.* As I splashed the remnants of last night off my face, I thought, *You dumb bitch. Your pussy just got you fired.*

I lingered in the shower. Soap across thigh—that felt better. I almost masturbated to get a release from the pent-up night. But then I had a dirty thought: *Save that cum for Jackson.* Which I did. I knew it would be an epic cum when he finally pulled it out of me.

I thought about not going into work at all. But on my office desk, I had a Polaroid-style picture of Jackson and me, taken on a roller coaster on our third date. Jackson the alpha dog is screaming like a little boy, holding onto me for dear life.

I wanted that picture. Oh, and there was Herman the Plant, which my friend Becca gave me before we had a falling out.

"You're always killing house plants," Becca told me before giving me Herman for my desk. "Well, you can't kill this one."

And it was true. I had forgotten to water Herman for weeks at a time. Herman could happily endure my travel schedule and somehow stay green. Anyhow, I wanted that plant, too. And I didn't trust Allen to send it all home to me in a thoughtful care package.

I drove to work in brooding silence. I half-expected a box of stuff to be waiting for me at security.

"Hi, Jameson," I said.

Our main door guy, Jameson, always gave me an extra stare as I walked up. Jameson was a nearly retired, jovial black man. He had a naturally flirty style and an easy confidence I liked. For some reason, I didn't mind him looking.

"Heya, Corrie!" Harold said. "How's my main squeeze today?"

"You mean your *other* squeeze," I scolded, in mock disapproval. "How is the old bird, anyway?" I was referring to his wife, Betty.

He cracked a smile from ear to ear.

"Jameson, did anyone … leave anything for me?"

He rummaged behind the front counter.

"Nothing I can see, Corrie! But if you want to squeeze on back here and look for yourself …." Jameson liked to press his luck.

I walked past him to the elevators, giving a big ol' hip swish on the way. Since this was probably my last time up, he might as well have something to remember me by.

"Okay, now!" Jameson called out, registering his approval.

On my way to the 11th floor, two of my co-workers filed into the elevator. They seemed to look at me a bit curiously, but maybe I was imagining things.

I passed our floor's receptionist, Yvette, on the way to my office. Yvette was on the phone and waved, not giving me a second thought. *Hmm* ....

That was when I looked over my left shoulder and noticed Allen's office—no lights on. That was odd.

Allen was a notoriously early riser. The latest he had *ever* showed up at the office was 6 a.m., as far as anyone knew. His secretary Gretchen had only beat him once. It was a running disagreement between them if he had indeed arrived at 6:01.

And here it was, 8:30. I unlocked my office. Nothing unusual. The sun was slamming in the windows.

I was still puttering around, checking to see if Herman was ready for a change in locale, when I heard my door creak open. My heart skipped, and then I almost fell over. Standing in front of me was Sirenna, in a brassy two-piece red suit. It was the first time I had *ever* seen her at the office. Next to her was Allen, but he seemed, well, a bit off. For the first time I could remember, he didn't have a tie on. His suit even looked disheveled.

Allen always had a cocky and defiant look—even last night he had looked more angry than submissive. But something had changed.

"All the way in, Allen." Sirenna motioned to him like he was a dog in obedience training. He shuffled into the room, and she closed the door behind him. "Allen has something to say to you, Corrie."

A long, awkward silence ensued. I was too numb from shock, I think, to say anything.

"You're … not fired." Allen said to me, before looking up. I thought I saw a flash of defiance, but then he was back to being sheepish.

"And what else, Allen?" Arms crossed, Sirenna was tapping her foot with impatience.

"I've put you in for a regional manager role," Allen said.

I had to sit down; this was a bit much.

"And …?" Sirenna prompted.

"It's kind of ... a custom role," Allen stammered, looking more at the ground than at me. "It's the consulting director part of my job. They'll be hiring a controller to handle the finance part. You'll still run your analytics group half-time."

"But ..." I said, wondering what the hell was going on.

"Allen has put in his two weeks' notice," Sirenna said. "We're moving to Los Angeles."

She was beaming. I couldn't help but think of *Mad Men*, when what's-her-name moved west to pursue her acting career. But Don Draper hadn't gone with her ....

"I'm going to pursue my acting career!" Sirenna said proudly. *Bingo.* "And maybe some modeling."

A moment of quiet while the absurdity of all this soaked in. I was glad I was sitting down, or I might have fallen over.

"And Allen won't be pressing charges against you or Jackson," Sirenna said sweetly. I felt her eyes gently scolding me, but not hating.

Sirenna looked ... different. Always a sensual woman, she was radiant now. With a swift movement she locked my door and closed the blinds. It was as it I was watching a movie of my life unfold, or maybe a reality show.

"Corrie, I want to show you something," she said. She pushed Allen up against the desk.

"Take your clothes off, Allen!" she said. He didn't move, so she repeated, "You heard me, Allen, take them off!"

There was absolutely no way Allen, this aggressive alpha dog motherfucker, was going to take off his clothes in front of two women, including his subordinate.

You could have knocked me off my chair. With a little bow of obedience, Allen started unbuttoning his dress shirt. Impatient, Sirenna helped him with his jacket, then tossed them both aside.

"The pants, Allen, the pants!"

It was odd, almost creepy, but Allen continued, as if under hypnosis.

"I've got your shoes," Sirenna said, quickly pulling Allen's brown loafers off until only his black socks remained.

By then, Allen was in his boxers. And I must admit, for the first time, I started to become aware that this scene was not just about his humiliation and my shock. I was starting to get turned on.

"The boxers too, Allen!" Sirenna said forcefully. It happened as if in slow motion. And suddenly there was Allen, standing up against my desk, looking wiry, white, a bit hairy, and ... naked. Except for the black socks.

Allen was covering his genital region, an automatic reaction you'd expect of anyone finding themselves naked in a forced/new situation.

Sirenna wasn't having any of that. "Allen, move your hands away! Don't make me do it for you."

Allen looked hesitant, but then I saw a new look in his eyes, a look that I am struggling to describe to you now, but it was as if a part of him wanted this to happen.

I was actually feeling bad for Allen, but when he moved his hands, I couldn't help but laugh. It wasn't just me; Sirenna laughed also. Jutting out from his pubic hair was a tiny little penis. It was inside of something—what was it?

"This is what Allen has been trying to fuck me with, Corrie!" Sirenna said. I was still in shock, worried to cross further lines with someone who in theory still had some level of power over me.

Sirenna seemed to notice my hesitancy.

"Corrie, I can assure you, nothing bad is going to happen to you. Tell Allen what you really think."

"What is ... on his dick?" I asked hesitantly, still testing the waters.

Sirenna stood next to him and reached down, stroking his tiny penis while Allen exhaled. "It's one of Jackson's condoms! You left one at my place, so I decided to see if it would fit. It looks like a little kid in a fat man's raincoat!"

I smiled; it was kind of true. Allen's little dick was almost lost inside this huge rubber, which looked more like a small plastic bag.

"I had to actually tape it on him so his dick wouldn't fall out on the way here," Sirenna said mockingly. It was true. Allen's condom was attached to the base of his cock with duct tape. *Ouch*, that was going to sting later.

"Can you believe he tried to cheat on me with this?" Sirenna said, stroking and pointing his little penis at me.

That reminded me … *Allen had cheated on Sirenna.* He had made my life miserable here. And I was hardly the only one.

"Your husband's cock is about ten times bigger than this. He made me cum so fucking hard! Imagine what this little thing can do for me. Nothing, Allen! Nothing!" She looked at him fiercely.

She was right about that. Jackson told me later, Sirenna had the deepest and widest vagina he had ever fucked. It was the only time he could ever recall "feeling a loose pussy."

"Allen and I have had a little talk," Sirenna said, stroking him with two fingers while she laughed. "A little tiny talk."

I can't lie; I laughed too.

"We're going to stay married, but now that I know how good sex can be, I'm going to be getting taken care of by other men. Isn't that right, Allen?"

"Yes," he said, not even hesitating anymore. I wish I had seen this before spending time with Brad. I had nothing on Sirenna in terms of taking charge of a short-dicked man.

"Oh, but there's more," Sirenna said. "Allen has an apology for you." She took her hand way. He looked at her desperately. "Oh, you don't want me to stop, do you?" He shook his head. "Then tell her!" Sirenna said.

"I'm sorry … I put you down and made your life hell here," Allen said.

Never had I known a man to completely renounce himself like this. Maybe Allen was under some weird spell, but he did look sincere. He had trouble looking me in the eye, but hey, I'll take a bizarre groveling apology over nothing.

"And why did you treat her like that, Allen?" Sirenna said as she stroked.

"Because …" he said. He stopped—but she stopped too—taking her hand away. He gave her that desperate look again, so she resumed stroking, and he resumed talking. "Because I'm threatened by you."

"And why, Allen?" Sirenna looked him the eye, forcefully.

"Because I know I could never please you."

"And why?"

"Because my dick is too small."

"Too small for Corrie?" Sirenna pressed, stroking harder. I could hear Allen moan.

"Yes …" he said.

"And not just too small for Corrie," she said, pulling her hand away. It was as if they had played these games all their lives.

"Too small for all women." Allen sighed.

"That's right!" Sirenna said, motioning me aside.

Allen bucked and squirted, shooting spastically into the condom.

"Oh sorry," Sirenna said. "Allen made a little tiny mess! Good thing we had this condom on you, Allen. You really can't control that little dick!" Then she looked at me again. "That's not the real reason we're here, Corrie."

What?

"We're here because, well, Allen has a favor to ask. Allen?"

Allen was finally tongue-tied.

"He really does have a soft spot for you," Sirenna said. "Allen, do you want me to ask her for you?"

Silence. Then, "Yes." Allen looked down at the floor.

"Allen is going to miss seeing you in your sexy outfits and trying to control you," Sirenna said. Allen looked ashamed but oddly content. He was shivering slightly, but it wasn't the right time to feel sorry for him.

"He was hoping you would … stroke him off one more time." Sirenna paused. "But there's more," she said after a moment. "He wants to know … how you really feel."

Sirenna took the big condom off Allen's penis, ripping the tape quickly while Allen moaned, and wrapped it in a Kleenex. Allen's tiny penis was still rock hard, evidently ready for more.

I felt one more moment of hesitation, but it passed. Sirenna had this situation under control, and to be honest, she had caught me up in it. It was like reading a shocking page-turner with an ending not yet revealed.

I quietly took off my jacket, as if stripping for a lover. My blouse came next.

"Ooh, you are hot!" Sirenna said. "Isn't she, Allen?"

Allen took a long, hard look, nodded, and stared at a spot on the floor again.

"No more clothes off, Corrie," Sirenna scolded. "Allen doesn't deserve it."

"No, he doesn't," I said, kneeling in front of him.

I figured after such a hard cum, Allen would be soft. But his tiny penis was trembling, jutting out hard for me. Using my thumb and my index finger, I stroked him again. But today I wasn't holding back.

"This is one tiny penis, Allen! No wonder you are such an asshole," I told him, then, correcting myself, added, "*were* such an asshole!"

Allen moaned, as if in a trance. I suddenly felt weird kneeling down in front of such a pathetic display of manhood, so I stood to his right and continued my stroking. Sirenna stood to his left, so Allen was totally surrounded by estrogen. Now I was in the zone. Everything I had done with Brad came rushing back.

"You could have made everyone's lives easier if you had just accepted your tiny penis," I scolded as I stroked. Already he seemed to be breathing heavily. "You should have let your wife fuck bigger cocks a long time ago. What were you doing cheating on her with such a tiny dick? You are lucky to have this goddess at all!" I looked him straight in the face. Although he evaded my eyes, the words were hitting home—I could feel it in his tensing body. I held him against the desk with my left hand while stroking with my right.

"He's going to watch me from now on," Sirenna said.

"Oh yeah, you're gonna love that," I taunted him. "Your tiny dick loves seeing your wife actually cum. We learned that last night, Allen, didn't we?"

Allen forgot to respond.

"Didn't we, Allen?" I said, pulling my hand away just as Sirenna had done.

"Yes," he said obediently.

"You're going to be nice to your female employees from now on, got it?" I said. He nodded meekly. "And you're *never* going to try to put this inside them!" Then I just lost it. "You could *never* please a woman with this tiny boy dick! I've fucked small guys whose dicks were about twice as big as this little guy, and guess what, Allen? I could barely feel them. You could never please me with this! I would never let your tiny penis anywhere near this pussy!" I realized I was yelling, maybe too loud. *Yikes!* I lowered my voice. "You're damn lucky this beautiful girl married you and put up with you. I wouldn't have even let you inside me once."

Then something came over me.

I stood up, took my skirt off, and rubbed his tiny penis against my panties. "You'd like to get inside this, wouldn't you?"

Allen moaned. I was surprised he didn't cum on the spot.

I could tell he was close to squirting—so pathetic. I had to let go of his cock for a minute. I wasn't done with him yet, not after everything he had put me through.

Allen was caught up in something he could barely understand, but it had considerable sway over him. He was now as hard as he was ever going to be, so I could get a good look at him. I couldn't help but laugh.

"You know you can't please a hot girl like Sirenna with a

tiny dick like this, right? Look how fucking small it is!" I could hear Sirenna laugh as well. It really was comical to learn that this powerful, grown man was so ill-equipped to deal with a sexually demanding woman.

I reached over and grabbed the end of my bookshelf, moving my ass up in the air, right next to his cock.

"Look at this ass, Allen ... look at it!"

Allen couldn't hold off and reached for his cock.

"No, Allen! No stroking! It's not time for you to come yet!" I scolded him. "Look at this ass, Allen! This ass you have stared at so many times. If I asked you to fuck it, you couldn't. You're too fucking small. Aren't you, Allen?"

Moans. This was the first time I had confronted him directly like this.

"Aren't you, Allen?" I demanded.

This time, a meek reply, "Y-yes ...." I had never heard him stutter before. This twist of events was so fucking satisfying.

"You shouldn't be mad at me for helping your wife get a proper fuck without divorcing you. You should be thanking me, Allen."

Sirenna looked happy. Hopefully this would keep Allen under her thumb for a long-ass time to come, knowing what other women really thought of him.

Walking around my desk, I had an idea.

"I was jacking you off with two fingers—two fingers, Allen! God, no wonder you are such an asshole. I'd be an asshole too if I had such a useless penis."

I reached into my desk for my trusty ruler. I had once used it to measure Jackson's cock right in my office. I came very close to begging him to fuck me right over the desk. Instead, I had written a "J" on it, right at the 8.5 mark. That was the biggest I had ever seen him, but then he was super horny that day, as it was his only blow job ever in my office.

"Let's measure that tiny dick. I want to see just how small it really is. Have you ever measured it, Sirenna?"

"No," she said. "He always told me it was average, like five inches."

"What? Five inches is *not* average!" I said. "And besides, there's no way this is five. C'mon, Allen, let's measure this tiny penis." I leaned the ruler against his pubic hair. Allen was larger than I was thinking—just over four inches. It was still fucking tiny. And it was *sooo* thin. I think that's why he seemed so incredibly small, even compared to the other little guys.

I rounded down out of spite. "Three point seven five inches, Allen. Wow!" I said.

Sirenna laughed. "Allen! You lied to me!" she laid into him, joking but mean.

"Look here, Allen. Here's the size of the last boyfriend I cheated on, with Jackson," I said. I pointed to just under six. "He felt so small in my pussy. And he was only five and a half … on a good day. Look at this J." I pointed. "That's Jackson's size!"

"Wow!" Sirenna said, kneeling down for a closer look. "Jackson is such a man!"

"It takes two hands to jack his cock off!" I said, kneeling down also. "Two fingers is all I need for you." I grabbed him to begin stroking again.

But then I had an idea. Sirenna had given me a huge break; I owed her something special, and I had just the thing. The shelf next to my desk had a bunch of small dolls made out of toilet-paper rolls. It was a crafts project my daughter had made out of found objects for school. One of the dolls had lost its head. I had two extra toilet paper roll centers stashed underneath my shelf, hoping to repair the sculpture before my daughter stopped by and noticed the headless doll.

Grabbing one of the extra toilet paper rolls, I turned to Allen and said, "Allen, do you know about the toilet-paper roll test?"

Allen shook his head.

"Well, I read about it online," I taunted him. "It's a good test a woman can use to see if her husband has any sexual right to her pussy."

"How does that work, exactly?" Sirenna asked, intrigued.

"Well, you simply put the empty roll on his dick," I said, standing over Allen. "And if his dick fits—and especially if it doesn't come out the other side—he has no business trying to fuck pussies."

Sirenna laughed. She could probably guess what was about to happen.

Sure enough, Allen's cock slipped right into that roll. You could see the very tip of his hole sticking out.

"No friction, Allen!" I said, trying to fuck his dick with the hole like a pussy. "You lose, Allen!" I had thrown all caution to the wind in my urge to dominate this motherfucker.

"See, Allen? You had no business trying to please your wife!" I said.

"Yeah!" Sirenna piled on indignantly, egging me on.

I started working the roll harder up and down his dick, but there really wasn't anything there, so it lowered and came off pretty easily. I actually almost slammed his penis into the roll, catching myself just in time.

"Do you know, I tried this with Jackson once," I said, looking Allen right in the eye as he stared back, then looked down, as if he had no right to meet my stare. "And guess what, Allen? The head didn't even fit! I couldn't even stick the end of it on Jackson's huge cock!" Okay, that part was a lie, but I did later test it on Jackson and sure enough, I couldn't begin to get the end of the roll onto him.

Allen moaned and I instinctively pulled the roll off of him.

"Oh no you don't!" I said. "You're not cumming on my work clothes! I don't need any more sperm in my eye!"

Sirenna laughed, likely at the memory of me spastically wiping Allen's cum from my eye the night before.

"Oh, little Allen is about to cum?" Sirenna teased. "Yeah, he never does last very long," she added with contempt.

I wanted to make Allen cum and cement my place deep inside his now-submissive head. But not at the expense of a squirty mess. I had an idea.

"Sirenna, do you have one of Allen's condoms in your purse?"

"No," said Sirenna.

"Hmmm ..." I said, rummaging around in my desk. I found some Crown condoms I had bought at a drugstore. These are the kind Olivia Munn was caught shopping for. I'd been curious to try them on Jackson because I knew from her talk show that Olivia loves big cocks. But the Crowns were way too thin for Jackson—they broke apart every time we tried to put one on.

I'd brought them to the office, thinking they'd make a good joke for an office party. I could pass them on as a Secret Santa or something.

"Allen, let's see how these condoms fit on you. They're useless for Jackson. This way you won't squirt all over my desk."

In a gesture of mock submission, I kneeled before Allen so I could focus on sliding the condom on him. I was genuinely curious to see how it would fit.

I pulled the condom out, surprised by its thinness. I'd forgotten how sleek the Crown condoms were—too sleek for Jackson. But on Allen, the fit was nice. Well, they were pretty easy to roll on, and there was plenty of room at the end. In fact I pulled the extra to the end of Allen's dick, leaving about four inches of slack.

Sirenna and I burst out laughing again. "Looks like Olivia Munn would be pretty frustrated right now, Allen," I said, looking up. He was confused by the reference; I didn't bother explaining.

I started stroking Allen within the condom, but to be honest, I was a bit disappointed. It was loose and ridiculous on him, but not ridiculous enough.

But then I remembered something. In my desk I had hidden a package of oversize condoms I'd ordered from overseas for Jackson. I was going to give them to him for his birthday in a week. Jackson had been complaining that the Durex XXLs he used were too tight on his dick, and he was always eager to take them off when we used them.

I'd recently found out that the U.S. has regulations for how wide a condom can be. But Europe doesn't. So, supposedly the best condoms for thick cocks are a European brand called MYSIZE. I ordered them on Amazon from a nice German couple, even corresponding with the wife about the sizes, discussing the wonders and problems of well-endowed men. I'd ordered a twenty pack of their widest and longest size (69mm wide, I think).

The condoms hadn't arrived in a box, so I was going to buy a special box for Jackson and give them to him for his birthday. I reached into my bottom desk drawer and pulled one out.

"Allen, I want to see how you fit into Jackson's new condoms," I said.

"Oh boy …" Sirenna said. "*This* I have to see."

She actually kneeled down as well and stroked Allen for a second, to make sure he was hard.

Then I was kneeling next to her: two sexy, fuckable women kneeling solely for the purpose of sexual humiliation.

"How long do you think Allen can last before he cums?" I asked Sirenna.

"Oh, I don't know," Sirenna said. "I'd say three minutes of stroking inside that condom."

"How about if I take my tits out," I said to Sirenna, pulling on my bra and buttons until my tits poked out in my dress shirt, kind of like we always wanted Kathryn Morris to do on *Cold Case*.

"Oh no!" Sirenna said. "Not much more than two minutes, I'd say."

"Honestly, Sirenna, I am insulted," I said. "Get your timer ready!"

Sirenna took her phone out and found a timer function. In the meantime, I got the condom out of the wrapper. I didn't put it on Allen's cock yet; it felt bigger in my hands.

"Five, four, three, two, one—go!" Sirenna called out, a bit too loud, even in this closed office.

With that, I took the condom and quickly rolled it onto Allen's cock. It rolled on super fast and super easy. I was amazed.

I quickly pulled out the slack.

"Wow, Allen!" I said, about to start stroking.

"Hold on!" said Sirenna. "I have to take a picture of this!"

She stopped the timer and took a couple of photos—I backed off a little to make sure I wasn't in the pictures.

My hand, with freshly manicured red fingernails, did appear in the side view, holding the tip of the condom away. It looked like Allen's penis was in some kind of huge, baggy plastic raincoat. At least six inches of plastic hung loose. Even compared to Allen in a Durex XXL, this was comical.

"Okay, let's begin again," Sirenna said, restarting the countdown.

I took the challenge seriously this time. It was hard to jerk Allen off in such a loose-fitting sack, but I quickly got the hang of it, using my thumb and two fingers to apply pressure, squeezing through the plastic.

"Jeezus, Allen, you are just swimming in Jackson's condoms!" I said, stroking him furiously while he leaned against my desk and rocked and moaned. I didn't bother telling him that Jackson hadn't tried them on yet. Turns out they were super nice and snug on Jackson, with just a bit of extra right at the end, which helped to catch his big cum-loads. I didn't know that yet, but I had a feeling ….

"Allen, look at your baby dick in here!" I said, putting his right hand on my tit.

He compulsively reached for it and moaned. I didn't care, I just wanted to fucking own him.

"Allen, even as a younger girl, I never stroked off a dick as skinny and small as this one. This is a little boy's dick. There is no way you can please a pussy with this little baby dick! I wouldn't let you anywhere near—"

Before I could finish, Allen grabbed my hand and groaned,

spurting hard into the condom and spasming against me.

"Oh my fucking god!" Sirenna said. "Twenty seconds!" Again, way too loud. "Your tiny dick couldn't last twenty seconds for a sexy girl like Corrie, now could it?"

"Well, he did cum a lot, I have to give him that," I said, carefully removing the condom and putting it in a napkin. It was way more cum than the night before. I suppose Allen's complete and utter humiliation really turned him on. I can't remember the last time I felt more powerful, more in control.

For the first time, Allen looked me in the eyes and didn't look away. Maybe he was taking a snapshot of this moment, one neither of us had ever imagined. But I didn't see the kindness I had seen in Brad's when I teased him, or in Daniel's before him—although I had never teased Daniel about his size, just other things. I saw a look of sexual satiation, a look of submission, but underneath, a flash of steely hate.

Somewhere down there, the real Allen still lived, and seethed. But this part—this new submissive part—this was real too. What would happen when those two parts collided? Could Sirenna survive those sparks? Thank god he wasn't my problem.

Post-orgasm, things got awkward and quiet. "We're gonna head out now, Corrie," Sirenna said, fetching Allen's clothes. He dressed quickly, in silence. Sirenna looked happy, at peace. Like she had conquered something … which I guess she had.

But I'll never forget that steely look in Allen's eyes, concealed by his newfound meekness.

"You be careful," I whispered to her as she followed him out.

Chapter 22

Last I heard, Allen and Sirenna were both alive, at least, and on the West Coast, although we made a point of losing track of one another.

I didn't want to tell Jackson about this little encounter.

For a while, I told no one. I went to work uneasily the rest of the week, concerned there would be consequences. I figured Allen was only in a temporary stupor and would wake up enraged.

But Allen never did come back to the office. Rumors about what happened persist to this day, along with some truly wacky stuff about Allen's sudden departure.

My co-workers never heard a peep out of me. Well, except at a girl's night out, when we were talking about the smallest penises we'd ever seen. ("I can't believe you actually measured it, Corrie!") But I didn't say whose it was.

Under duress or not, Allen did give notice, and I got my promotion. I even got his secretary. She's been giving me some knowing looks and the occasional funny smile, but I'm not saying squat. Now my job is about proving I can handle everything on my plate. That I deserve this chance.

Once I knew the promotion was official, I told the family. Chelsea gave me a big, happy hug. All I could think was, *You don't know the half of it, girl!*

Then I told Jackson the other half.

He was almost shocked. But not quite. It was obvious I had been jolted into a change. He was all for it. Somehow, that bizarre scene opened me up again. Maybe the shock peeled my defenses away, or showed me how fragile all this really is. I don't know. But Jackson and I are lovers again, not just sluts for each other. I can't keep my hands off him, but we're kissing like prom dates, too. I really should have a talk show!

If you're thinking I never let Jackson fuck another man's wife, you'd be wrong. I've accepted that part of my fate—and his. But I did make some changes. First off: the husband *always* has to agree. He doesn't have to watch—that's up to him. Jackson doesn't mind these restrictions one bit. He pretty much got his cake and his icing too, and that sweet son of a bitch knows better than to question his good fortune.

Weeks go by as a normal married couple, but I always have my antennae up. Usually the wife is the one who approaches us, but not always. When it comes to female ecstasy, the grapevine is pretty powerful. But even if the wife starts the ball rolling, I insist on meeting with the husband on his own before anything happens.

Some of the wives don't like that, but by then they are already pining for Jackson. And if not, I know just what to say. They relent. And yes, it's always married women. I think that keeps the whole thing cleaner. I remain haunted by Lisa, who was technically single; our friendship didn't recover. I also find it incredibly hot to see the lengths wives will go to—literally—to get the sexual fulfillment their husbands cannot provide.

Their urgency and desperation for Jackson always sparks our own sex. Watching husbands' eyes glaze over in jealousy, frustration, humiliation, and yes, relief—that remains a fascination.

In the year since, Jackson's fucked five more wives. So, yeah, we're still up to no good. But we pace ourselves. I don't know how to express exactly how I feel about the situation, but I'm less compulsive about it now. If it started as a late night fix; now it's the life we share.

Don't get me wrong—it's still hot as hell. Nothing beats watching a wife get the best fucking she's had in years. The ones who have never been fucked like that are the best.

Recently we seduced a wife who is a local newscaster, so I can't say her name. In her innocent sex life of four partners, she'd never had a dick much bigger than five inches. Her generous husband knew she was missing out. She had the tightest pussy Jackson could remember since high school. For once, he had to take it slow, slow, slow. But she opened up—they always do. I wish you could have heard her grateful screams. I'm touching myself just thinking about it.

But here is the weirdest thing: if we do this the right way, it seems to make the marriages we encounter better, not worse. That may sound bizarre, or maybe self-serving. If you think so, there's not much I can say to change your mind, I guess.

One thing I do know: if two people love each other enough, they can make almost anything work. If they bring the whole truth, not just the convenient parts. If I pick up on any weirdness in a potential couple, we back off. I don't want to tie anyone down against their will again. Nor do I want to make a bad marriage worse.

I do miss bringing assholes like Allen down to size. But we have a strict "no jerks" policy now. I do let my domme side out, when I know the scene is safe for everyone. I tell the husbands that the only thing I can promise them is intense pleasure for their wives, and that they need to be ready for what that will feel like.

Other pressures go away, though. The husband is off the performance hook. He is so relieved to stroke and watch and not try to do things to women his little dick wasn't made for.

And a well-fucked wife makes for a happier home; we all know that.

If they face it together, they can have some intense fun along the way—and, as I've now learned, come out the other side the better for it.

As for salvaging my own marriage, Brad actually helped me with that one. And that's the weird part. As much as this strange adventure with Jackson brought our marriage to a better place, it's my friendship with Brad that carried me over.

With Jackson these days, sometimes I'm his wife, sometimes I'm his slut. Sometimes I'm his lucky bitch who gets to fuck what all the other wives wish they were fucking. And yeah, sometimes I'm his pro bono pimp, watching him turn girls into happy puddles.

I finally got it through my exceptionally thick skull: Jackson is my gifted lover and companion; he's not everything I need in a man. In Brad, I found something I couldn't get with Jackson.

I think Cindy and Jackson are both a little uncomfortable with my friendship with Brad, but we make a point of only having lunch and only meeting in public places. We found a hole-in-the-wall breakfast place that has a halfhearted lunch crowd. We can sit in the back and speak frankly.

It's usually not about sex; it's about other stuff. Brad is just so open with his emotions. And he seems to understand my odd mix of badass goddess and little girl seeking comfort.

I've made a point of being brutally honest throughout this little memoir, so I'm not going to tell you I have it all figured out. But I think Jackson and I are going to make it.

Sometimes, when Jackson and I have a dispute, I look forward to my weekly lunch with Brad a little too much. I find myself wishing Jackson had the grasp of his own psyche that Brad has forged.

Which brings me to Daniel.

One day, about a year after all this went down, I was walking into the parking lot after a lovely lunch with Brad. I got into my car and drove, impulsively, toward where I knew Daniel lived—he moved back about a year ago, but we both agreed to keep our distance.

Driving over to Daniel's, I found myself wondering if he was single.

Then I had the craziest thought: *What if you got this all wrong? Should you have married Daniel, and let Jackson be your lover?*

It was a potent, distressing thought. I flipped on the radio but the Foo Fighters' "Best of You" was on, and that only made the moisture turn into tears.

Then I had that thought again: *Should you have married Daniel?*

At the time, I had eliminated that option. Sex with Jackson was life-changing, amazing, and Daniel and I were flat-lining.

But that was back when I assumed marriage came in one vanilla flavor. Now I knew better. Next came the deviant idea: *The same honesty that worked between me and Jackson could have worked with Daniel.*

If I had told Daniel I needed other men to please me sexually and wanted to share that adventure with him, would he have agreed? Would he have been open to it?

Would he have loved me all the more for it? And would he have loved my dominant side, which I don't exercise with Jackson but would have been compelled to act out with him? Would the honesty have been enough to spark us? I believe that it would have ....

Dammit Corrie, if only you'd had the guts to be honest with him!

The tears kept running as the memory of Daniel's kind eyes lingered, how close I'd felt to him. It wasn't that simple, of course. I told myself, *You didn't know then what you know now.* But the missed opportunity gnawed.

I'll never know what would have happened to me, or Jackson, if Daniel had been home alone that day.

As I drove by his corner, I saw him there, but not alone.

A pretty woman with a small child was outside with him. It looked like the woman was trying to track down a wayward cat, but the cat ran up a tree and she slipped, muddying her sundress.

There was laughter and … a kiss.

Not a long kiss—it was a family type of day at Daniel's place—but a kiss nonetheless.

I kept driving. I would learn through a mutual friend that I had seen Daniel with his future wife and her son from a prior marriage.

I don't know if Daniel is happy, but he sure seemed that way, at least that day. I ran into him one more time, just today actually, at the same spot where Brad and I meet. I introduced Dan to Brad, who had the good grace to say he'd heard a lot about Daniel. Daniel looked curious—he's one smart dude—but he left it alone.

We only spoke for a moment—"how are you?" type pleasantries—but something did happen. As I looked into Daniel's eyes, I could see a warmth, a forgiveness. It was a forgiveness I didn't deserve, but I'm grateful to Daniel for finding it in his heart.

Once upon a time, I faced two doors, each leading to very different lives. I took door number two. Like Gwyneth Paltrow in *Sliding Doors*, a part of me wants a do-over, wants to see the other side and where it would have taken me. Far from where I am now? Or would I have arrived at the same place?

I would wreck my life if I tried to open that other door now. I'll never know what it's like to be married to a Daniel or a Brad. I wound up with a different set of marital tradeoffs.

Just like Jackson has a gift for women, I have a gift for the husbands that come our way—a gift that might strike you as strange, cruel even. These are sweet, likable men. But they are struggling. Their liberation lies in embracing their submission, a certain kind of blameless inferiority that balances their strengths.

Or so I tell myself. Granted, my tactics are taboo. But one thing I do know: when we have these adventures with Jackson, it's not just the woman who is liberated. Yes, the woman gets a gratifying release, but I've learned something very surprising: the husbands need it more. And I don't just mean sexual catharsis. Yes, the good-hearted ones love to see their wives in ecstasy, but it runs deeper: they need it for themselves. They got stuck playing "normal nice guys," whereas I think their true path is both more submissive and fiercer. And yeah, far more intense. But you know that part by now.

I'd like to think that I helped Brad pass through to a stronger, more accepting place. At least that's what he tells me. It feels so much better to help Brad than to tear an asshole like Allen down. So as this confessional ends, maybe we can count that as my emotional progress.

I hope I can reconcile my longing for kind/submissive men with my marriage. I hope I can be a devoted wife without losing something primal I crave almost as much as love. I guess I'll find out.

ALEX HATHAWAY, ALSO THE author of *From Housewife to Cuckoldress* and *Education of a Cuckold,* is fascinated by the erotic power of sexual taboos and the adventures that can be had by exploring them. An author whose relationships have evolved from vanilla to anything but, Alex has a particular interest in writing about cuckolding and the unconventional sexual fulfillment it can provide.

Fanny Press offers a choice selection of cuckold erotica by Alex Hathaway, Rob Matthews, David McManus, and Derrin Hart. For more information, go to www.fannypress.com.

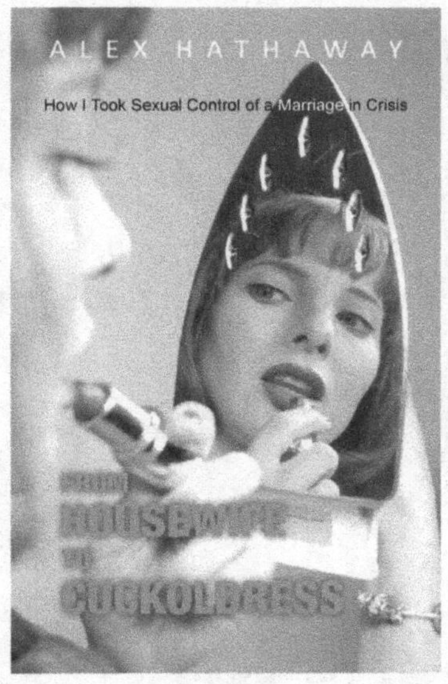

A woman's earth-shattering encounter with her best friend's supremely well-hung lover sets her on a quest to reassert her sexual power. But how long will her pliant, poorly endowed husband be willing to go along for the ride? Is it really in his nature to play the willing cuckold or is his resentment building? A portrait of a very modern marriage.

Jason falls hard for his high school friend Beth, but he isn't confident enough to make his move. When Jason discovers Beth's secret—she is sexually voracious—he also realizes he is too poorly endowed to satisfy her. But wait … watching her with other men is no small turn-on. Finally, as an adult, he meets Kristen and begins to take his extracurricular studies in submission seriously.